Beautiful Disasters

Beautiful Disasters

Kendal Lou Dickson

CONTENTS

This book is dedicated to Kat.

Thank you for looking out for me when life felt hopeless. I would not be here without you.

We may not be close anymore, but you will always have a special place in my heart.

"There is no perfection, only beautiful versions of broken-
ness." — Shannon L. Alder

A MESSAGE TO THE READER

Dear reader,

I hope that you enjoy these short stories, as I have written a little bit of myself into each piece.

Please note that some of these stories include difficult topics such as abuse, violence, and self-harm. Reader discretion is advised.

I ask that you kindly leave a review via Amazon or Goodreads once you've finished the collection.

Thank you for your support,

Kendal Lou

1

Awakening

A heavy fog hangs in the air. Light rain pelts the ground. Thick oak trees line the rocky path that runs adjacent to a shallow stream. The only source of light is being provided by the beams of the full moon. The ground is mushy. Two men, Greg and Josh, canvass the wooded area. They are cousins and roommates. Greg suggested this impromptu hunting trip a few days ago. Midterms start on Monday, but Josh can't take anymore long nights cooped up in the campus library. He knew if he read one more article about the anti-Semitic elements in *The Merchant of Venice* he was likely to take a pound of his own flesh. He also needed an escape from his clingy girlfriend, a fashion design major, who does not understand the point of studying for exams or how distracting a flood of text messages can be.

"Hey, Josh. I need to take a piss. You go on without me. I'll catch up," Greg says.

"Roger that," Josh says.

Josh walks towards the stream, his old *Ariat* boots sticking with each step. As he kneels to replenish his water bottle, Bass retreat from the water's edge. He pulls down his scarf, the cool wind brushes against his bearded face. It stings his cheeks. He checks his watch, 02:14 AM glows on its face. Greg and he have been out in the woods since midnight. They have not seen any deer yet, only their tracks and a few coons. An owl coos in the distance. The night air aches. Josh pulls his wool beanie down tighter on his head, hiding the blonde wisps that were peeking out. He shudders as the wind sneaks under his jacket.

Rustling sounds from across the stream make his heart race. Cautiously, he takes a few short steps back from the edge. He has no time to retreat farther. Hopefully, with the abundant fog Josh will not need more cover. He grabs his Winchester and crouches down. A doe appears, and a smile creeps onto Josh's face. The winter has been kind to the deer, her body is filled out and fleshy. Drool puddles in his mouth. He can already taste smoked venison. Cradling the barrel with his left hand, Josh presses the butt of his rifle against his shoulder. His body is tense. His finger shakes as it hovers above the trigger. The deer approaches the stream, seemingly unaware of his presence. She lowers her head for a drink.

The brush moves behind the doe. A small fawn, adorned with white speckles, clumsily joins her at the stream. His finger hesitates on the trigger.

***

Josh waited for his mother on the curb in front of his elementary school. His fingers fiddled with an origami crane he had made. The edges of the paper bird were taped down. He did not trust his own folding abilities to prevent the bird from returning to its original state, a square piece of orange construction paper. The sun was beating down on his head. One-by-one he watched his classmates leave with their mothers. He looked at his plastic watch. Fifteen minutes past three. His mother was never late.

A hand touched his shoulder and his face lit up. He looked up, expecting to see his mother's beautiful face; however, it was his teacher, Miss Butterfield staring down at him. His smile faded. Her pale pink lips were pursed. Behind her stood Josh's uncle, Jimmy. His eyes wildly dashed from his teacher's face to his. Uncle Jimmy never picked him up.

"Josh, your uncle Jim is here to pick you up today," Miss Butterfield said.

His mouth fell open. His mother never allowed him to spend time with this man, especially unsupervised. She told him it was because he was always busy with work. Josh was only ten, but he knew better. Uncle Jimmy's son always showed up at family reunions with his arms peppered in purple and blue bruises.

"W-where is my mom?" he asked.

Miss Butterfield broke eye contact and pulled her hand to her face. An uneasy feeling budded in Josh's stomach. As stood up, Uncle Jimmy stepped forward. He was a large, stout man that towered over him. He placed his calloused hand on Josh's shoulder.

"I think you two should go somewhere private to talk," she said.

"No. T-tell me right now," he said.

Uncle Jimmy squeezed his arm roughly. Josh pushed his hand off, making his face turn red.

"She was in a car accident," Uncle Jimmy said.

***

A gunshot rings out. The doe raises her head and looks straight at Josh. She and her fawn bolt. *Dammit.* He stands up, brushing the mud away from his pants. He lets out a long sigh before taking a sip of water. A howl pierces the night, raising the hairs on Josh's neck and sending a cold shiver down his spine. He rubs his forearms. Leaves crunch behind him and he turns around. A silhouette of a man is limping towards him. The man's head is limply resting on his shoulder. His right leg is being dragged to the left. Josh's squints to see through the fog.

"Are you ok?" Josh asks.

Slowly the man shambles into the moonlight. It is Greg. Josh's mouth falls open. Greg's hand is pressed on his neck, blood seeping through his fingers. There are multiple slashes across his chest and torso. His once hunter green jacket is now deep crimson. Greg's right foot, now bootless, is contorted sideways. He crumbles to the ground. Josh rushes to him.

"Greg! What happened?" his voice squeaks.

Josh holds him in his arms, carefully supporting his neck and head. He coughs, and blood spews from his chapped lips. His breaths are heavy.

"I think I ran into a bear, I don't know. One second I was standing, the next something knocked me down and was on top of me... I shot it, but it didn't die... it just ran off and I came to find you," he says.

What? How? Josh's eyes wildly intake his surroundings. *Did it follow him here? Are we in danger?* He tries to speak, but nothing comes out. Panic paints his face. Another ghastly howl shrieks in the wind and Greg's eyes widen. He wildly scans their surroundings.

"Josh... Josh, I need you to focus. We need to get out of here," he says.

Josh's eyes fall back to him. Greg's hazel eyes are locked on him.

"Just give me a second to think here," Josh says.

He rubs his forehead, drawing his eyebrows together. *It is a fifteen-minute hike back to the trail, and it will probably take us another twenty to get back to the truck. I don't even know if he can stand.* He digs for his phone in his pocket. The only thing his fingers find is a small hunting knife. *Shit. I must have left it in Greg's truck.*

"Do you have your phone?" Josh asks.

Weakly, he shakes his head no. *Of course, the first rule of hunting trips: always leave your phone in the car.* He bites his lip. The air is still around them. Greg's face is wincing in pain.

"Do you think you can stand?" he asks.

"I can try," Greg says.

Josh stands up, clasping Greg's hands in his. Greg allows Josh to pull him up, pressing weight on his left leg. He tries to balance on both feet. He utters a cry, staggers, and buckles. Josh's grip prevents him from falling down completely. His bottom hits the mud with a soft thud. Tears glaze over his eyes. A low growl echoes off the tree trunks. Greg trembles uncontrollably, his hand tightens around Josh's forearm.

"You need to get out of here, now," Greg says.

"I'm not leaving you," he says.

A twig snaps behind them. Heart pounding, Josh reaches for his rifle. His eyes strain to see in the moonlit fog. Two amber circles glow like nightlights. He takes a deep breath and squints harder. There is a shadowy outline of a massive creature. It looks like a bear. *Shit.* His eyes frantically look to Greg and then back towards the unknown creature. Greg is hyperventilating. His hand is clenched on Josh's pant leg.

Sweat beads on Josh's forehead. *No matter what, carrying Greg or not, I cannot outrun a bear.* Josh aims his rifle at the shadowy outline of the massive creature. His hand shakes, his aim is off. *How am I going to shoot it if I cannot see? Maybe firing off a few rounds will scare it off.* The creature starts barreling towards Greg. It is not a bear.

***

Josh paced in the kitchen. His fists were balled. A fruit fly buzzed by his ear. It must have been drawn by the pile of dirty dishes in the sink. Food, cooked weeks ago, was caked on the plates. Nervously, Josh looked at the wall clock. Seven o'clock. Uncle Jimmy would be home soon. Josh pounded his fists onto the grey counter top. Greg walked into the kitchen. He stood in front of Josh, placing his hands on his shoulders.

"Calm down, Josh. You only skipped one class, and I already erased the message on the answering machine. I doubt the school bothered to call his cellphone," he said.

Josh's looked up at him. He was eighteen, only four years older than him, but he was far wiser. *I doubt he would ever skip Algebra for a girl. Especially a freshman girl who already slept with the entire junior varsity football team within a month of the school year. I wish I was as smart as him.* The front door blew open. Goosebumps rose on Josh's arms. His heart was pounding.

"Josh? Where are you boy?" Uncle Jimmy bellowed.

Josh swallowed. Frozen with fear, he cannot speak. Uncle Jimmy flew into the kitchen. His wild eyes scrambled before focusing in on him. His face was bright red. A vein bulged in his neck. Greg stood in front of Josh.

"Get out of the way son. This is between me and the boy," he said.

Greg stood his ground; his feet were firmly planted on the white tiled floor.

"I said get out of the way," he spat.

Warm liquid ran down Josh's leg. He was shaking uncontrollably. Greg does not budge.

"Leave him alone, pop. He just missed one class," Greg said.

An angry cackle erupted from Uncle Jimmy. He slapped his own knee.

"He did not miss, he skipped. Principal called, said they found him in the locker room, pants down with a girl on her knees," he said.

Josh felt like he was shrinking into nothingness. *I want to disappear.*

"He is just a kid, come on, you are overreacting," Greg said.

Uncle Jimmy raised his calloused hand, and he slapped Greg. Greg fell against the counter. A red hand mark was imprinted on his cheek. Jimmy turned his attention to Josh. He closed his eyes. A crash echoed against the cream-colored walls, but Josh felt nothing. He opened his eyes. The kitchen table was overturned, along with two of the chairs. Greg was lying against one of the chairs, its pine leg was broken in two. Blood oozed from his hooked nose. Uncle Jimmy stood over him. His right hand held Greg up by his shirt collar while his left was drawn back into a fist. Defiant eyed, Greg stared at his father.

Josh stood there, in a small pool of his own piss, unable to move. Uncle Jimmy plowed his hand into Greg's face. Repeatedly his knuckles met Greg's high cheekbones. Each hit made Josh wince. Still, he did not move. He wanted to yell for him to stop, but he cannot. He was too scared.

***

The moonlight reveals its ghastly appearance. It is larger than a full-grown male grizzly bear. It has ears and a snout like a wolf, but its body is long with muscular features similar to a human. Stiff, steel grey hair covers it entirely. Greg utters a high-pitch cry as it pounces on him. It begins tearing at his bloody torso with its sharp canines. Josh is frozen in place. Terror, confusion, and disbelief paralyze him. Somehow, through his redundant thoughts of *what the fuck is happening*, he manages to fire a shot at the beast. Hair flies as the bullet pierces through the creature's shoulder. It growls and turns its attention from Greg to Josh. It stands up on its hind legs, throwing its massive paws into the air before leaping towards Josh. He has no time to shoot again, only enough time to hold the gun sideways in front of him, bracing for impact. The creature knocks Josh down onto his back. It presses its mangy neck into the barrel of his gun. It is heavy. Josh's knuckles are white. Saliva bubbles on the creature's lengthy tongue. Its snapping jaw reaches for his throat. Putrid breath invades his nostrils, the stench brings a tear to Josh's eye.

Its massive paws are digging into the muddy earth on either side of Josh. His arms begin to throb. Snarling, the beast pushes more weight against him. *I cannot keep this up.* He closes his eyes. He feels like he should start praying but he can't. Josh stopped believing in God when his mother died. He could never praise a God that stole such a kind soul from his orbit, replacing her with an abusive monster. A monster who did not think twice before clobbering his own son, let alone his nephew. He pictures Uncle Jimmy's red face as he yells at him. His breath reeks of whiskey. Greg stepping in between them, taking a hit. A hit that was meant for Josh. Regret overcomes him. *I never stood up for him, but he always came to my defense. I was such a coward then. Fuck, I still am.*

Greg's mutilated body flashes in his mind. *If I die here, right now, what will become of him? Will this thing finish him off or will he be left to bleed out? A few miles off the trail, it could be weeks, maybe even months before anyone finds our remains. I cannot let this happen. I cannot die the coward my uncle made me out to be. I am better than that. I am better than him. I refuse to give up. I just need is a distraction. Something.* Josh's eyes widen. He remembers the knife in his pocket.

The beast redirects its attack, clamping down on his left forearm. Its sharp incisors puncture through his jacket's thick sleeve and into his skin. He opens his mouth to scream but nothing comes out. It feels like he is being stung by a thousand bees. Josh drops his rifle. It falls to his chest. Gritting his teeth, he reaches for his pocket. Adrenaline, like a rush of electricity, pulsates through him. Josh's hand meets the blade. Mustering the remainder of the strength he has left, he plunges the knife into one of its amber eyes. The creature releases his arm. It cries out an eerie screech. He has his chance.

Josh kicks the beast's hairy chest. The force pushes him away from his adversary. The creature scratches at its eye. It whimpers, and paws at its mangy face. The knife is no match for the beast's curled claws. It falls silently to the ground. The beast focuses its attention back to Josh. He cannot breathe. It feels like time has crippled him, his movements are slow. He aims the gun at its chest and pulls the trigger. The force of the bullet sends it back on its haunches. It turns away, attempting to escape as another bullet whizzes into its shoulder. The gun jams when he tries to shoot it a third time.

It would not have mattered if his gun had even gone off the third time. The creature is already fleeing. Even with a limp, its great strides swallow the earth. In an instant, it disappears into the forest. Josh's ears are ringing. *What the fuck just happened?* His body is shaking. His arm is now numb and is no longer stinging, but it is bleeding profusely. Josh tears his jacket off. The beast's teeth tore through his skin as if it was wax. He strips the scarf from his neck and ties it tightly above his elbow. He catches Greg, unmoving, out of the corner of his eye.

"You...you alright buddy? It's gone," he says.

Greg offers no response. Josh crawls over to him. He places his fingers on Greg's neck, checking for a pulse. Nothing. Josh lays his head over his heart. Silence. He pulls his head up and looks at Greg's face. His eyes are glassy and empty, the life has completely evaporated from them.

"Greg, oh no, please no" he chokes.

Tears well up in his eyes and begin cascading down his rosy cheeks. He lays his head on Greg's chest and begins sobbing.

"I failed you, I'm so sorry," he says.

Snot runs down his upper lip. His body is quivering. He is all alone now, Greg was all he had. Greg was his everything. Images of Greg flood his mind, from their first Christmas together after his mother's death, to their many Saturday nights spent cat-calling girls at the local bars. His heart aches, the air has vanished from his lungs. He pictures Greg shaking him by the shoulders, telling him to pull his ass together, the fight isn't over yet.

"But I can't do it without you," he says.

He knows if Greg was here, he would have laughed, his dimples showing before he reminded him, 'You just fought off a fucking werewolf, yes you can.' He takes a deep breath and pulls his head up. He looks at Greg's face. Josh wipes his nose on his sleeve.

"You're right... I can, I owe it to you, I must," Josh pauses as he wipes the blood from Greg's chin, "I'm g-going to take you home, buddy."

Josh is dizzy, but he somehow manages to stand up on his weak legs. He picks up Greg's body, cradling his cold cousin in his arms. His arm throbs under the weight. *I need to get back to the truck and retrieve my phone. Maybe this scarf will hold up long enough for me to get help.* His feet struggle as he walks uphill, the ground is slippery. The full moon taunts him. Most of the fog has dissipated. The rain is now a heavy drizzle. All he can think about is the beast. Every time he closes his eyes, he sees it. Its glowing eyes staring back at him and into his soul. The stench of the creature's breath still plagues his nose. *How am I going to explain this to the authorities? Uncle Jimmy? He's going to fucking kill me.* Josh sighs. His stomach is churning. The cheeseburger and fries he had for dinner bubbles up his throat. He swallows the burning liquid chunks. It is uncomfortably quiet. No owls, no squirrels, just the occasional rustling of branches and his footsteps. A howl echoes in the wind, making his spine tingle. He fights the urge to howl back and quickens his pace.

Awakening was first published in Mercy: A Short Story Collection in March 2019.

2

Lifeline

I t's three o'clock in the morning. The San Francisco temperature struggles to rise above fifty degrees. The sky is pitch black; thick clouds cover the stars. A man in his early twenties stands at the edge of the Golden Gate Bridge. His thin body quivers, not because he is cold, but because he fears what comes next, if anything.

He's never been religious. Maybe that's what's wrong. Maybe God could have helped with the piling student loans, the inability to make it past the first interview, or the overcast shadow of loneliness that has grown far beyond his control. It's just become too much to bear. Everything feels insignificant, meaningless, hopeless.

Small waves crash against the bridge's support columns. A few cars blur by, but other than that the man is utterly alone. The bridge itself is quiet. He takes a deep breath, hands caressing the red railing in front of him. *One jump and this will all be over.* His heart beats steadily, pitter-pattering like raindrops. He throws his leg up. The rubber sole of his tennis shoe grips the rail. His hands clench the steel as he pulls his other leg up.

He carelessly stands up. The wind kisses his boyish face, reddening his cheeks. He is no longer trembling. Relief and excitement pulse through his veins. He can taste the freedom of death on his tongue. Its sweet finality calls to him as if it was a siren and he a sailor. He stretches his arms out as he casts his head back.

"Stop! What are you doing?" a voice says.

Caught off guard, the man struggles to keep his balance. The upper-half of his body teeters towards the water. His rubber soles slip. He no longer feels in control and it frightens him. Someone wraps their arms around his legs from behind, steadying him.

"What are you doing? Let go of me," he says.

He looks down, straining to see in the dark. He can make out a boy, maybe eighteen or a little younger. The round face is panic-stricken.

"M-my name is H-Henry... please d-don't do this. I don't know what you're going through, but this is not the answer," the boy says.

The man on the railing sighs and rolls his eyes.

"Please just leave me alone."

He tries to wiggle his way out of Henry's grip, but it's no use. Henry's fingers dig in through his stiff denim and into his skin. He groans.

"Screw off kid. This doesn't concern you. You don't even know who I am," he says.

Henry's grip tightens. He shakes his head. Tears are budding in his eyes.

"It doesn't matter. I can't just sit by and watch you do this. I couldn't live with myself if I did," Henry says.

"Then don't watch," he snaps.

Tears stream down Henry's cheeks.

"Do you really think the world is going to be better off without you? What about the people you'll leave behind? Do you know what this will do to them? Do you even care? You can't seriously be this selfish."

"Are you kidding me? Do you think I'm up here on a whim? That I didn't think about it for months?" He pauses, gritting his teeth before adding, "Do you think I would be up here if I had people that cared about me?"

"I care about you," Henry says.

"You don't even know me," he says.

"What's your name?" he asks.

"It doesn't matter."

"It does to me."

A police car drives past behind them, sirens screeching and lights flashing. A fire truck, follows closely behind, horn bellowing in the night. Neither speak as the noise fades away into the darkness.

"What's your name?" Henry asks again.

'Noah," he whispers.

"Nice to meet you Noah. Why don't you step back and talk to me for a little bit?"

"Why? You can't change my mind," Noah says.

"Maybe I can, maybe I can't. It's only hopeless if you don't let me try," he says.

Noah takes a deep breath. His mind is heavy. Only a few minutes ago, freedom was within reach. He could almost touch it with his fingertips. Now it feels as if it is an eternity away. *Maybe if I humor him for a few minutes he'll leave.*

"Fine, but you're going to have to let go of me first," Noah says.

Henry cautiously loosens his grip. A sigh of relief escapes his chapped lips as Noah turns himself around. He offers his hand. Noah takes it, pressing his hand to his, stabilizing himself as he steps down.

"Alright. Let's get this over with," Noah says.

Henry throws his arms around Noah's neck, almost pulling him over as he embraces him. Noah's face flushes as his arms wrap awkwardly around Henry. Their hearts pound in unison. Henry's cologne, strong and earthy, overtakes him. His warmth, comforts him. For the first time in almost a year, he doesn't feel alone. Air catches in Noah's throat and he sobs into Henry's shoulder. His legs shake. His knees buckle, but Henry holds him steady.

"I'm not going to let you go," Henry whispers.

"I...I don't think I want you to," he says.

Henry and Noah sit across from each other at a corner booth in Denny's. The round clock on the wall reads four-thirty. The inside of the diner is almost vacant. A man, flipping through the Sunday paper, sips coffee several tables away from them. *Heaven* by Warrant softly plays over the speakers.

Henry reaches across the table and places his hand over Noah's. Noah fixes his dry eyes on the stack of blueberry pancakes in front of him.

"How do you feel?" Henry asks.

"I don't know... confused, I guess," Noah says.

"About what?" he asks.

Noah shrugs. Their waitress, an elderly woman with a permanent I-hate-my-job scowl, walks towards the table. Her jaw pops as she smacks stale gum between her false teeth. She goes to speak but Henry shakes his head at her. Seemingly attune to the tension between Henry and Noah, she turns around without a word. Noah presses his fork into a pancake. He's hungry, but his stomach is queasy, making him hesitant to eat.

"Why did you stop me?" he asks.

Henry takes a deep breath. He pulls his hand away and into his lap. Pain lingers in his eyes. He fiddles with his jean pockets, pulling out a worn brown leather wallet. He sets a faded photograph onto the table and pushes it towards Noah. It is a picture of a high-school aged boy. He is smiling a crooked grin and his brown eyes are squinting in the sunlight. The edges of the picture have white creases from being folded.

"That's Eli. We grew up together. He was my best friend," Henry says.

"Was?" Noah looks from the photograph to Henry.

Henry stares down at the table. He takes a deep breath.

"Yes, was. Eli committed suicide two years ago. He overdosed on his mom's sleeping pills." He pauses and makes eye contact with Noah, "It was unexpected. I mean, he had been acting strangely for a few months but not in the way... I mean maybe there were signs that I missed. He was my closest friend and I failed him."

"I don't know what to say," Noah says.

Henry shrugs. He wipes away a lone tear before it can slip down his cheek.

"There's nothing to say. I failed him, but I won't fail you." Noah scoffs.

"What?" Henry asks.

"No offense, but spending a couple of hours with someone, regardless of how nice they are, is not enough to change my mind. Besides, I'm not your friend, you can't substitute me for Eli," he says.

Henry slides out of the booth and scoots next to Noah. He takes both of Noah's hands in his own.

"It's not only going to be a couple of hours. I'm here for you, indefinitely. And I know you're not him. Saving you won't bring him back. But I owe it to him to be there for you, like I should've been for him. Here." He removes the cross necklace that was hidden under his grey Golden Gate University sweatshirt and clasps it around Noah's neck.

"This was Eli's. I want you to have it. It'll be a constant reminder that you're not alone."

Noah shakes his head.

"I can't take this. I don't even believe in God."

"The only thing you need to believe is that I'm here for you now, and always, whether you want me to be or not. You're not alone, not anymore," Henry says.

Noah smiles faintly. Henry leans towards him. their foreheads press together. Noah's cheeks blush. His heart races.

The warmth radiating off Henry's skin brings an unfamiliar sense of comfort. The waitress clears her throat, startling Noah. Henry turns to the woman, glaring.

"Do you boys need anything else?" she asks.

"No ma'am, we're fine," Henry says.

The waitress pushes her glasses up on her thin nose. Her wrinkled face is plagued with a mix of curiosity and annoyance. Noah refuses to look up until the woman retreats to check on her only other customer.

"Now what?" Noah asks. His voice is barely a whisper.

Henry smiles widely.

"You're going to finish your food and then we're going home," Henry says.

"I don't want to go back to my apartment... there's too many reminders there of what's going wrong in my life right now," Noah says.

His eyes fall back to the untouched pancakes. A lump grows in his throat. A feeling of discomfort bubbles up in his stomach. Henry squeezes his hand.

"Don't worry." He waits until Noah looks him in the eyes again, "We're not going back to your apartment. We're going to mine."

Lifeline was first published in Mercy: A Short Story Collection in March 2019.

3

A Simple Mistake

"I think I drank too much," Greyson says.

He's hunched over as he walks, leaning on his friend and dormmate, Frederick, for support. Frederick, a tall and lanky twenty-two-year-old, is a student at the University of Michigan. A journalism major, he is never seen without the small leather-bound journal his grandfather gave to him before he passed away. His brown curly hair is hidden by a plain, yellow baseball cap. Greyson is slightly shorter than Frederick, but they share similar features and could easily pass for brothers.

"You know, you didn't *have* to drink those last two shots," Frederick says.

"But, they were a gift. It would've been rude to those dolls had I not," he stops and throws his hand over his mouth, "I t-think I'm going to b-be sick."

Greyson pulls away. He rushes to an alley behind an old building that appears to be an abandoned store. Its red bricks are faded and instead of the missing shingles being replaced, the gaps were covered with boards.

Frederick sighs. "Yeah, right, it would have been rude.

He checks his watch. Two o'clock. *Dammit Greyson*. He walks towards the alley. A poster on the window of the store catches his eye. He doesn't know enough German to make out what it says, but he knows from the Swastika it's some form of propaganda bullshit. Frederick reaches for the poster but hesitates. Weariness overshadows him. He looks to the left, and then right. The night is silent minus Greyson's heaving. The sidewalk is vacant, and no car engines are running. He yanks it off. Part of him wants to keep it, bring back to America to show his three brothers how bad things are in Germany; however, he knows better. Hand on each corner, he tears the poster in half before shredding it into tiny confetti-like pieces. He lets it slip through his fingers.

Feeling a tap on his shoulder, Frederick jumps. It's only Greyson, but his heart rate refuses to settle down.

"I want to go home now."

"What? You don't want to spend your last night in Germany partying? That wasn't your mood earlier."

Greyson shakes his head. His freckled face is pale.

"That was quite a few drinks ago."

"I know," Frederick slaps his friend back, "I'm just teasing."

The interior of the motel is as quiet as the outdoors. A bellhop sits in one of the lobby's plush chairs. He's skimming through the Berlin newspaper.

"Guten Morgen," Frederick says.

The man's eyes meet Frederick's, but he doesn't say anything. An apathetic expression is on his elderly face. He returns his attention to the newspaper.

Frederick helps his friend to their room. Their professor, Dr. Bowman, and two other classmates are asleep in the room next to theirs. The room is small. A single, full-sized bed is pressed against the wall. The only other furniture in the room is a nightstand. Frederick's journal sits on the nightstand along with a half-empty glass of tap water. Greyson kicks off his shoes and crawls into the bed. Frederick goes into the bathroom. The mirror reflects bags under his hazel eyes. He strips down to his boxers and gets in the bed next to Greyson, who is already snoring. Frederick closes his eyes.

Frederick wakes up. Someone is banging on the door. There's shouting in German. Groggily, he checks his watch. It's only seven in the morning, too early for anyone to be awake since their flight out isn't until noon. He sits up in the bed and rubs his eyes. Greyson is still asleep.

He shakes Greyson's shoulder. "Hey, wake up."

Greyson stirs, mumbling something under his breath. Suddenly, the door flings open. Heavily armed Nazi soldiers rush into the room. The barrel of a Karabiner 98K is shoved into Frederick's face. His body breaks out in a cold sweat. Greyson comes to. He tries to sit up but is immediately pushed back down in the bed by a soldoer. His eyes wildly dash around the room.

"Frederick, what's going on?"

"I-I... d-don't know."

The soldiers part and make a path as their general enters the room. The Nazi is somewhere in his mid-thirties. His face is stone-cold, and his shoulders are broad. He walks straight up to Frederick and says something in German.

Frederick opens his mouth to speak, but he can't. There's a massive lump in his throat. Tears are welling up in his eyes. The general repeats what he said, his tone is harsher this time.

"W-we're from America. We s-speak English," Greyson says.

A soldier whispers something to the general who raises his hand in the air. A scrawny, older man walks into the room. He isn't wearing a Nazi uniform, but a Swastika is embroidered on the chest pocket of his shirt. The general exchanges some words with him and gestures to Frederick.

"Are you Greyson Jackson?" the older man asks.

Frederick slowly shakes his head. He looks to Greyson. They exchange a worried glance.

"I'm Greyson."

The man turns to the general. He whispers something, ineligible. The general strokes his stubby chin.

"Nimm ihn," he says.

Suddenly two soldiers grab Greyson. He cries out. Their fingers dig into his upper arms as they pull him from the bed.

"Let go of him!" Frederick yells

He grabs at Greyson's arm, but a soldier hits him in the face with the barrel of his gun and he falls back. Blood oozes from his thin nose. He places his hand over his face.

The soldiers drag Greyson out into the hallway and slam the door. Frederick frantically slips into his jeans. He rushes into the hallway. The voices of the soldiers echo throughout the hotel. He bangs on the door next to him. No answer. He opens the door, it's vacant. The bed sheets are thrown about the floor. He nearly trips down the stairs as he runs towards the lobby. There's a small crowd of guests pressed against the windows. On the outside of the hotel there are photographers, reporters, and news vans. The spectators gasp as Greyson is thrown into an unmarked Gestapo car.

It's overwhelming. Frederick feels like the air has been knocked out of his body. He trembles. A cold sweat covers his half-naked body. Camera lights flash. The soldiers are circled around the building. They shout and push the bystanders back with their guns pressed in front of them. There's a hand on Frederick's back. He turns, Dr. Bowman is standing behind him. The fifty-something-year-old professor is tall and thin. Metal-rimmed glasses are pushed up on the bridge of his nose. His skin is pale, whiter than a sheet.

"Frederick, go pack your things, and please pack Greyson's as well. I'm arranging for you, Matt, and Brad to go ahead and go to the airport."

"What about Greyson?"

Dr. Bowman shakes his head. "I don't know, yet."

Everything is blurring together. Frederick doesn't remember getting dressed or even packing, but he's now sitting in the lobby with Matt and Brad while Dr. Bowman speaks to the hotel attendant. Matt is eighteen, the youngest of the group, and appears to be as frail as he is short. Brad is in his mid-twenties, but his brown hair is already greying. Frederick clutches his journal in his trembling hands. His eyes are glued to the floor. The events from the morning won't stop replaying over and over again in his mind.

"I can't believe he did that," Matt whispers.

"Yeah, I thought he knew better," Brad says.

Their words pull Frederick from his thoughts.

"Did what?" Frederick asks.

The two classmates exchange a wary look with one another.

"Sometime last night," Brad lowers his voice, "he stole a propaganda poster."

Frederick's stomach drops. "He did what?"

Brad motions for Frederick to lean in closer.

"Apparently he was really drunk. A shop owner saw him take a propaganda poster and rip it up," he looks at Frederick, who's sweating again, "hey, weren't you with him last night?"

"Please excuse me, I need a moment."

Frederick drops his journal as he rushes out of the lobby and into the outside air. It's sunny, but chilly. His body slumps over the yellowing grass. He can't stop the warm liquid chunks from spewing out of his mouth.

"Are you ok?"

Frederick manages to stand up. Dr. Bowman is standing beside him. Frederick shakes his head.

"Listen, don't worry, I'm sure I can get Greyson out of this mess."

"He's innocent."

"I'm sure he is. He may not be the sharpest tool in the box, but he wouldn't do something so *stupid*," he looks up and down at Frederick, "you don't look good. Did you drink too much last night?"

He shakes his head. "I didn't even get tipsy, but...*something did happen.*"

"Now is not the time to confess about bringing a girl into your room or something miniscule like that. My focus needs to be on Greyson."

"This is about Greyson..."

"What? Do you know something?"

Frederick nods. There's a suffocating lump in his throat. He opens his mouth, but he cannot say the words. *It was me. I took the poster off. I should be the one needing help, not Greyson.*

"Hey, the bus is here to take us to the airport," Brad interrupts.

Frederick looks to the street. He hadn't even heard the bus pull up. Matt stumbles out, suitcases under both arms and in both hands.

"Frederick," Dr. Bowman captures his attention again, "was there something you wanted to tell me?"

"No sir."

Dr. Bowman scratches the back of his neck. "Alright then, go get yourself on the bus."

Defeated, Frederick takes his bags from Matt and walks to the bus. There's an overwhelming feeling of guilt and shame hanging over his head. *Maybe Greyson will get out, he IS innocent. There's no way they will convict an innocent man...right?*

"Wait, don't start the bus!" Dr. Bowman shouts.

Frederick's heart stops. *Did the bellhop say something to him?* Dr. Bowman rushes into the doorway, panting.

He's holding Frederick's journal. "You almost forgot this."

Frederick takes the journal. He feels a slight sense of relief, but the guilt refuses to waiver. *This is my last chance...*

"Um, Dr. Bowman?"

"Yes?"

He breaks eye contact. "Take care of him. Make sure, he gets home safely."

"I promise I will, don't worry."

Frederick couldn't sleep or keep anything in his stomach during the ten-hour flight home. His mind just kept replaying the events of the morning and the night prior. He didn't talk at the airport or even on the drive back to the university. He walks through the dorms silently as he pulls his suitcases.

"You've been awfully quiet since we left the hotel," Brad stops walking, "is everything ok?"

"Not really. I'm worried about Greyson," he says.

Brad frowns. "I am too."

"Guys... come here," Matt says.

Brad and Frederick trade glances before going into the common area of the dorm. There's a small crowd of co-eds surrounding the small television set. The running headline on across the screen says, "U.S. college student involved in fatal accident overseas".

"Hey, turn it up," a guy says.

"Alright, hang on."

"University of Michigan college student Greyson Smith died today in a fatal car accident in Germany," the anchor pauses momentarily, "Greyson was in custody amidst allegations of theft, and property damage."

An image of an overturned Gestapo car appears on the screen. Frederick covers his mouth. He can't hear anything besides the deafening thuds of his own heart. The faces of those around him are skewed, resembling the Nazi soldiers that had taken Greyson.

"It should have been you," one soldier says.

"It should have been you," the other soldiers chant in unison.

Frederick covers his ears with his hands, to no avail. The soldiers keep getting louder, repeating 'it should have been you' over and over again, like a broken record. Tears well up in his eyes. Eyes tightly shut, he falls to his knees.

"Stop it! STOP IT!" he screams.

"Frederick, what's wrong?" Brad asks.

He opens his eyes. Everyone is staring at him. The Nazi faces are gone, and the room is quiet. Frederick slowly stands up. His legs are wobbly.

"Frederick?"

"I... just need to go lie down," he says.

The crowd watches him as he walks away. Brad follows closely behind. He feels dizzy, but he manages to make it up the stairs and to his room. His hand is too shaky to use the key.

"Here, let me," Brad says.

He takes the key from Frederick's hand and unlocks it. The air conditioning welcomes his clammy skin. The room is small, fitted with two beds, a small kitchenette, and a bathroom. Greyson's side of the room is decorated in camouflage.

A picture of a black lab is framed on his nightstand. Frederick's side is plain. His bed is covered by a brown comforter. Several books are messily thrown on the ground. There's a picture of Greyson and Frederick, standing in front of the dorms both wearing smiles, pinned on the wall.

"Are you going to be ok in here by yourself? I'm sure we could get you moved into another room," Brad looks at Greyson's bed, "or I could even sleep in here and you could stay in my dorm."

Frederick shakes his head. "I'll be fine. I just want to be alone, if that's alright."

"Ok... just know I'm here for you if you need anything."

Brad closes the door behind him. Frederick walks over to his bed. His fingers trace the edges of the photograph. Tears slide down his cheeks. He grabs a pillow from his bed and throws it across the room. Greyson's scared face flashes in his mind. He crumples to a heap on the floor.

"It should have been me..."

A Simple Mistake was first published in Mercy: A Short Story Collection in March 2019.

4

Broken Promises

The door to the apartment is never unlocked. She didn't think too much about it, assuming Nate was probably scatter-brained after his late-night shift at the hospital. The blinds are shut, and the curtains drawn. A disheveled stack of papers sits on the kitchen bar. The only light is coming from under the bathroom doorway. A long-haired tabby cat sits on the outside of the door, its right paw extended under the door frame. Maisie checks her watch, 11 o' clock in the morning, too early for him to be awake. She sets her backpack on the serape print couch and walks into the kitchen.

"Nate, you up? You want something to eat?" she asks.

No reply. She sets out the white bread, and retrieves honey-smoked turkey from the fridge, along with other sandwich fixings. Nibbling on a potato chip, she walks to the bathroom door. The feline looks up at her and releases a yodel of a meow.

"Easy there Cheeto."

She tosses a chip crumb to the cat, but it's not phased. She makes three small taps on the door.

"Nate? You didn't fall asleep in there, did you?"

No answer. She touches the door handle, it's locked, something unusual. Like a small spark igniting, a feeling of uneasiness is forming in the pit of her stomach. She knocks thrice more, harder this time, but still, no answer. The cat meows again. She stands on her tip toes, her red acrylic nails grasping for the key above the door. Silently it falls to the plush carpet. Her eyes are drawn to the corner of the door. Scratch marks. Messy lines of light tan are engraved where the white paint normally is. Her body breaks out in a sweat. Suddenly, she doesn't want to open the door.

***

Maisie walked into the bedroom. A pink satin gown clung to her small frame. Nate was lying in a queen-sized bed. Attired in a long sleeve t-shirt, reading *It*. Cheeto, only a small kitten, sat at the edge of the bed.

"Aren't you hot in that?" she asked.

He shook his head, still buried in his book. Maisie flipped on the fan and crawled into bed next to him. His red hair was damp, stuck to his forehead. Sweat stains were under his armpits.

"Are you feeling ok?" she asked.

Nate sat the book down. "I'm fine. Why are you asking?"

"It's the middle of August and you're in a long-sleeve shirt. Last winter, do you remember what you wore when you had to shovel snow to help Mrs. Bailey get her car out? A t-shirt, and shorts."

Nate shrugged his shoulders. He refused to make eye contact with her. She touched his forearm and he winced.

"This is the third day in a row that you've worn that shirt, and every night you sweat, I can feel you next to me." She pulled her arm away and looked at the floral comforter. "Are you hiding something?"

"No, I'm not. Here, I'll take it off, it's no big deal."

With great care, he pulled off the shirt. Maisie gasped. Her stomach fell. His arms were zig-zagged with fresh scars, barely scabbed over.

"What?" he asked.

"What happened to your arms?"

He shrugged his shoulders. "They're just cat scratches."

"Are you fucking kidding me? He's a KITTEN, there's no way Cheeto did that."

Startled, Cheeto fled the room. Maisie ignored the sick feeling in her stomach and ran to the bathroom. She pulled out the sink drawers and frantically dug into them. Nate walked up behind her.

"What are you doing?"

Tears welled up in her eyes. "Where is it?"

"I don't know what you..." he stopped.

Maisie was staring him dead in the eye. He took a deep breath.

"I threw it out, after." Maisie resumed rummaging through the drawers, ignoring him. "Mais, I swear. I realized I shouldn't have done it and regretted it immediately..."

Maisie stopped. She stared down at the messy drawer. Nate touched her arm.

"W-why did you do it?" she asked, her voice barely above a whisper.

Nate's eyes fell to the floor. "I don't know, I've just been under a lot of stress lately. I misread a patient's chart last week, he had an allergic reaction to the pain meds I gave him... he nearly died."

Maisie crossed her arms. His words echoed in her head.

"Why didn't you tell me?"

"I was ashamed. I love what I do, but sometimes I feel like I'm drowning. What if I'm not cut out for this? What if he had died?"

A few tears slid down his freckled cheeks. Maisie cupped his face in her hand. She kissed him softly.

"There is no one more cut out to be an ER doctor than you. You are the most kind, caring, and empathetic man I've ever met.," she rubbed a tear off his cheek, "You can't beat yourself up about this. All you can do is be more diligent, work harder, use this as a lesson... but no matter what happens, you cannot hurt yourself."

"I know, it was stupid. I won't do it again. I'll even talk to the school counselor, if that'll make you feel better."

"You promise?"

"With all my heart."

***

Relax. He probably just fell asleep in the tub. She takes a deep breath, unable to fool herself with optimism. She doesn't remember picking the key up, but it's in her hand. She rolls the smooth copper. It's cold. It slides into the knob and with a turn to the left, there's a click.

"Nate, I'm coming in ok?" her voice is barely above a whisper.

The door creaks as it opens. *Has it always creaked?* Her heart rate is well over one-hundred beats per minute as she steps inside. The master bathroom is small and cramped. Two sinks are stationed in front of a long mirror. A small, claw-foot white bathtub that sits in the corner, and a toilet is catty-corner to it. There's water covering the blue tile floor. It soaks into her sandals as she steps inside. Forcing down the lump in her throat, she turns her attention to the bathtub, the source of the water. The image she sees doesn't automatically register in her brain, it's like a nightmare or a cruel trick of the eye.

Fully dressed in his scrubs, Nate lies in the bathtub. The water is muddied with blood. His skin is paler than normal, his lips are parted, and his eyes dull. One of his hands floats at the top of the water, the other hangs off the side of the tub. There's a deep gash to each of his wrists. A small razor blade, tinted crimson, lays on the tile.

"No...no... Nate, what, what did you do?"

Tears stream down her cheeks. The color has drained from her face. She releases a wail and falls to her knees. Trembling, she takes his hand in hers. His fingers are cold, but limp. She extends her other hand to his jawline, fingering his neck. No pulse.

Someone knocks on the door.

"Maisie, Nate, are you guys ok?" a voice says.

Maisie turns her reddened face from Nate. She opens her mouth to speak, but nothing comes out. Four more knocks are heard. Maisie struggles to stand. Her legs feel as consistent as gelatin. She manages to wobble to the door. From the knees down, her pants are soaked and tinted a pale red. Shakily, she grasps the knob, and opens the door.

It's Otto, a fellow student of the nursing program, and a close friend of Nate's. His eyes and hair are the same shade of chocolate brown. He's wearing navy-colored scrubs. A piece of paper is clenched in his right hand. His eyes travel from Maisie's face to her knees. His mouth falls open.

"Did he?"

Maisie breaks down again. Otto awkwardly puts his arms around her. Her hands are limp at her sides. Besides knowing each other through Nate's stories, they had only met about a handful of times.

"Where is he?" he whispers.

Maisie points a shaky finger towards the bedroom. Otto pulls her aside and walks towards the bedroom. The bathroom light is still on. He pauses in the doorway. The crumbled piece of paper falls from his hand. He gags, somehow able to prevent the throw up from escaping his chapped lips.

He looks to Maisie. "Did you call anyone?"

She doesn't say anything. It feels like her voice was stolen. She tries to take a step towards him but can't. The room is spinning.

"Maisie?"

Without a word, she falls to the ground, unconscious.

Maisie wakes up to the sound of strangers' voices. Her eyes flutter slightly before fully opening. She's on the couch with a thin blanket over her.

She jolts up. "Nate?"

Otto rushes to her. She tries to stand, but he gently pushes her back onto the couch.

"Hey, easy there. You've been out for a good bit."

"Otto, where's Nate?"

Otto's eyes fall to the ground. Maisie's eyes widen, she cranks her head around, there's three police officers standing in the kitchen. The image of Nate's floating body flashes in her mind. Tears well up in her eyes. An EMT walks out of the bedroom, pulling a stretcher with a body bag on top. Maisie jumps up, knocking Otto back. She runs to the stretcher, her hands grasp at the zipper. She pulls it down enough to see his pale face, now colored with soft hues of blue.

"Stop!" Otto grabs ger arms, his fingers digging into her flesh.

She crumples into his arms, sobbing. The EMT zips the bag back up, giving a sharp but empathetic look to Otto. Maisie keeps her eyes shut as Nate's body is wheeled from the apartment. Otto sits her down on the couch again, before bringing her a class of water. Shakily, she brings it to her lips. Her head is aching terribly.

A police officer brings a kitchen barstool into the living area, setting it a few feet across from her. He's probably in his mid-to-early thirties. His hair is a soft blond.

"Mind if I sit?" he asks.

She shakes her head. He sits down. A notepad is in his left hand, a black pen in his right. Otto sits down next to Maisie. His hand caresses her back.

"Can you state your name and your relationship to the decease-...to uhm... Nathan?"

"He went by Nate." Otto says.

The officer's face flushes. "Right, Nate, I apologize."

"M-my name is Maisie Williams. Nate is," she chokes back tears, "was, Nate was my boyfriend."

The officer scribbles on the paper.

"Did he ever express the desire to commit suicide, or do anything that might have led you to believe he was suicidal?"

She swallows a lump in her throat. "Yes."

Otto looks to her, he's tearing up.

"He... cut himself once, but it was almost a year ago, and he's been seeing a counselor every Tuesday evening, you can call the school and verify."

Otto's face drops. "They won't...be able to verify that."

Both the officer and Maisie look at him. He pulls his hands to his lap, fidgeting with his fingers.

"Every Tuesday, Nate and I went to the Watering Hole, up on second street," a tear rolls down his cheek, "I... I didn't know he was supposed to be seeing a counselor. We just shot pool and drank a few beers."

Maisie puts her face in her hands, slumping over. The officer silently jots down his words.

"Yet, you said earlier he gave you the note?" the officer asks.

Otto nods. Maisie sits up.

"Note? What note?"

"Officer Magellan has it. Hey, Magellan, can you bring the note here?"

Officer Magellan, a short and stout man, walks over from the kitchen. In his chubby fingers is a plastic baggy with a piece of notebook paper inside. Cautiously, Maisie takes it in her hand. With the speed of dripping honey, she opens the bag and unfolds the paper.

"Dear Otto,

I don't know what I'm doing, all I know is that I won't I can't do this anymore. My grades are slipping, Dr. Roberson is threatening to take me off rotations, and my financial aid is running out. It's like everything is falling apart at once and no matter what I do I can't stop it. I was planning on asking Maisie to marry me, I bought a stupid ring I couldn't afford, but I now know that's not fair to her she deserves so much better. This is probably going to be hard on her, but she will, in time, get over it... she has to. Please take care of her. I love you bro, thanks for always being there for me for everything.

Nate"

***

"Do you have any eights?" Nate asked.

Maisie shook her head. "Go fish."

It was a Monday afternoon. Maisie and Nate, who was absent of his usual scrub attire, sat across from each other at the kitchen table. Red backed playing cards were scattered on the table. Cheeto sat in a vacant chair beside them, all four paws folded up underneath him.

"Got any twos?" she asked.

Before he can answer, Maisie broke out in a coughing fit. Her cheeks reddened and her throat itched. Nate rushed to the sink, filled a glass with water, and handed it to her. Carefully, she took a sip.

"Thank you."

He nodded. "Anytime."

Maisie took a deep breath. Fighting a stomach bug, it was first day in a week she had felt well enough to attend class. Still, it was probably too soon. Nate pressed the back of his hand to her forehead. She was burning up.

"Are you feeling ok?"

"Not really, but I think I'm just tired," she took another sip of water, "I probably overdid it today."

"Why don't you lay down for a bit? You can rest while I run to the store."

"Alright, if the doctor insists."

She stood up and with his arm wrapped tightly around her waist, Nate assisted her into the bedroom. The bed was welcoming, but the room was too warm for her already sweating body. She pushed the covers away as Nate walked out of the room. He came back with the glass of water and a cool, damp cloth. Gently, he placed the cloth on her forehead.

"I know we're out of saltine crackers. I was planning on getting some stuff to make soup, but would you want me to buy some canned soup instead?"

"Whichever is easier."

"No, what do you want?"

She smiled faintly. "You and I both know your chicken noodle soup puts Campbell's to shame."

"Noted. I guess if nursing doesn't work out, I can always pursue a career as a chef."

They both chuckled.

"You're too good to me," she pressed her hand against his cheek, "how did I ever get so lucky?"

He shook his head. "Nah, I'm the lucky one."

He leaned in and kissed her. For a moment, she forgot she was sick. That was the affect he had on her.

"Is there anything else you need before I go?"

She shook her head. Nate stood up and pulled the sheet to her chest before kissing her again.

"Will you always take care of me?"

"Of course."

"You promise?"

He smiled. "Cross my heart."

Broken Promises was first published in Mercy: A Short Story Collection in March 2019.

5

Mercy

It is a quiet, foggy spring morning. It is so foggy, in fact, that only the tree tops are visible from an aerial view. The interior of Winter Grove, an asylum for the criminally insane and a home for the intellectually retarded, mirrors this dreary weather. Room 213 is small like the others. This room with its four walls, white originally but now yellowing, house the asylum's most intriguing patient. Nero Mikene, a twenty-six-year-old man, has been at Winter Grove for fifteen years. He was admitted for murdering his drug-addicted mother and abusive step-father, after a judge decided he was not guilty by reason of insanity.

Nero sits on the thin-cot in the room. The only other object in the small room is a bucket which serves as a makeshift toilet. Like the other patients, he wears a plain grey cotton shirt with matching pants and thin white slip-on shoes. His pale hand runs down his angular jaw-line and stops at his chin. He's waiting. Waiting for the orderlies to shove medication down his throat and then to be herded like livestock with the other patients towards the cafeteria, as per usual. Footsteps echo through the bleach saturated hallway. The steps seem to stop right outside his door.

Finally. He hears faint voices on the other side of the padlocked, steel door. Sounds like Regina, the head nurse. She is older, probably in her mid-fifties, and stout. Her face is wrinkled from a lifetime of hardships and her demeanor is similar to that of a Rottweiler. Nero cannot recognize the other female voice. It is softer.

Suddenly, the top of a head is visible in the bullet-proof glass square on the door. The face, or what can be seen of it, does not belong to Regina. It is a brunette with heavy bangs and large green eyes. When the eyes lock with Nero's mismatched eyes, his right blue and left brown, the head quickly ducks back down. *Great, another spectator.* Nero runs his hand through his long black hair before shaking his head.

More footsteps are heard followed by screams from other patients that are being released from their cages, one by one. The lock clicks and the door opens to two men. The male nurse, Jacob, is tall and lanky. He is only in his early thirties, but he is already balding. His face is kind, but he has recently lost compassion for the patients. Probably due to the fact that last week one of the patient's bit off a nurse's finger, sending her to a hospital. Nero doesn't know what happened after she was rushed away, only that she never returned. The orderly, Mark or something, has never been anything but cruel. He acts like he enjoys his job a little too much.

"Alright, after your last session Dr. Chaucer increased your dosage of diazepam," Jacob says.

He hands Nero a small plastic cup with colorful pills inside. Nero looks at the drugs and sighs. The head psychiatrist, Dr. Phyllis Chaucer, is always adjusting his medications and switching his electric-shock-therapy and hydrotherapy routines. She always tells him, once he gets better he will be able to leave. She dangles that in front of him like a fisherman dangling a worm on a line. It is always just out of his reach.

Nero thrusts the cup to his chapped lips and swallows the powdered concoctions. He opens his mouth, a habit now, allowing Jacob to ensure that he isn't hiding one of the pills under his tongue.

"You're free to go with the others now," he says.

Nero brushes past the two men and falls in line with the other patients as they shuffle towards the cafeteria. The smell is potent, bleach mixed with urine and feces. Nero is used to the smell but his eyes still water from time to time. The walk from the patients' hall to the cafeteria is short. The cafeteria is down the rubber-coated stairs, and to the left of the main entrance into the asylum. Having the entrance nearby is like another dangling object, but the doors can only be opened from the inside with a key. Only a handful of orderlies and nurses have the key.

The cafeteria itself is one of the largest rooms in the facility. Plastic picnic tables are crammed next to each other in several rows. Crimson stains, most likely blood and not ketchup, are permanently ingrained on the table tops. No amount of scrubbing or foul-smelling soap seems to suffice in order to whiten the plastic again. Next to the cafeteria is the recreational room. It is furnished with faux leather couches, plastic chairs and tables, and a ragged book shelf. The door leading out of the recreational room is unlocked, but it leads to a grassy area enclosed by a chain fence topped with razor wire. The one-time Nero attempted to climb said fence the wire wasn't kind to the palms of his hands, leaving him with ugly scars.

An orderly hands Nero a Styrofoam tray. The contents it carries are practically inedible. Stale toast with aged butter, mushy applesauce, and two boiled eggs are given as breakfast every day of the week. A single plastic spoon accompanies the tray, as patients are no longer given sporks after a girl with bipolar disorder stabbed a nurse in the neck with one. It wasn't a fatal attack, but it was serious enough to give the nurses a good spook. Nero goes to an empty table and sits down by himself. There are thirty-eight patients at the asylum, but none that he actually cares to associate with.

"Can I have your attention please?" Regina asks.

Nero stops prodding his bland applesauce and looks up. Regina is standing at the edge of the cafeteria, next to a new face. All the nurses are wearing white dresses, featuring a crimson cross, white stockings, and flat, white shoes. The unfamiliar girl is toying with the hem of her dress, apparently nervous. Judging by her chocolate bob and green eyes, Nero assumes she could be the one who was outside his door earlier. Her face is slender, fair, and unblemished.

"This is Farrah, our new nurse. She grew up taking care of her disabled brother and mother and has graduated from a prestigious medical school. I know that you will treat her with the utmost respect," Regina says.

There is a unanimous hello by the patients, making the young nurse's lips form a gentle smile. Nero looks to Farrah and their eyes lock. A soft red tint flashes on his cheeks, before he turns to his attention back to his unappetizing meal. He takes a bite of the applesauce, flavorless, as usual. Before he can take another bite, Nero feels a hand on his shoulder.

"It's time for your session with Dr. Chaucer," a male says.

He turns around. It is the same orderly from this morning, the one who upon closer inspection of his embroidered name-tag, is after all named Mark. Nero stands up and pushes the man's hand from his shoulder with a scowl. Even though Nero is somewhere over six feet tall and towers over him, Mark is not intimidated. His over-sized ego makes up for his lack of height. Mark chews an unlit cigarette between his browning teeth as he leads towards the stairs.

Nero follows Mark up two flights of stairs and through the nurses' hallway, stopping at the door on the far end. In gold letters 'Dr. Chaucer' is etched on the door frame. The orderly knocks softly and waits to open the door until a voice within calls out, "You may come inside."

The office smells strongly of potpourri, a stark contrast to the usual bleach odor. There is a large pine desk in the center of the room with a chair, one fabric clad and stuffed while the other plastic and plain, on either side of the desk. The top of the desk is bare, probably to ensure no patient goes rogue and attempts to use a writing utensil or paperclip as a weapon. Shelves are positioned against two of the four peach-colored walls. The shelves are stocked with boxes of patients' files dating back as early as 1954, only a few years before Nero's arrival. The back wall is home to two large windows, they are unbarred but crafted from bulletproof glass in order to prevent suicidal attempts. The wall by the door is decorated with Dr. Chaucer's certificates and scenic pictures torn from interiors of different travel magazines.

"Please, have a seat," Dr. Chaucer says.

The psychiatrist is in her early fifties, but dresses like she wishes she still is in her thirties. Her blood colored hair is stiff with hairspray, thick hoop earrings are visible under the hair strands. Dr. Chaucer's thin face is powdered two shades too dark and her cheeks are painted a peachy orange.

"What do I owe the pleasure of seeing you so soon again?" Nero asks.

His charm is amplified, he's suspicious of the unscheduled session. Phyllis's lips are pursed, seemingly unamused by his antics. She pulls a syringe from her desk drawer and places it on the top of the desk.

"Do you know what this is? Or where we found this?" She asks.

Nero nervously glances at the syringe before resuming eye contact. He shakes his head. Dr. Chaucer sighs and rubs her wrinkled forehead.

"This sedative was found embedded deep in the lining of your cot. Do you want to explain what it was doing there?" She asks.

Nero grinds his teeth together. He had not expected anyone to find the sedative nor had he prepared an excuse beforehand.

"Were you harming yourself again?" Dr. Chaucer asks.

Before Nero can answer, Mark grabs his arms and thrust them onto the desk. The underneath of both of Nero's arms are scarred heavily, puffy pink slashes from his wrist up to his elbows; however, nothing is fresh. Nero yanks his arms back down to his sides and shoots a glare at the orderly.

"How can you not be certain it wasn't planted?" Nero asks.

Dr. Chaucer sends Mark a look, something of the 'give us a moment' nature, and the orderly exits the office.

"Don't be coy. We both know you put the syringe there. The question is why? Now if you can tell me that I won't have to add additional sessions and prolong your stay at Winter Grove," Dr. Chaucer says.

This hits a nerve. Perhaps the single nerve Nero has left. He rises and slams his fist on the desk.

"Shut-up. Just shut-up. It doesn't matter what I do, or what I say. I could find the God you believe so much in and you still wouldn't let me leave!"

Mark rushes into the room, sedative in hand, but Dr. Chaucer raises her hand to stop him. Nero's outburst didn't affect her calmness.

"That's enough for now. Nero, please wait outside the door while I speak with Mark for a moment before he escorts you outside," she says.

Anger pulsates through his veins. Nero brushes past the orderly and slams the door behind him. In the hallway, grief and panic overtake his anger as the realization of spending eternity in the asylum settles in. Hopelessness radiates from his pores. Drawing back his pale fist, Nero throws it against the plaster wall leaving a dent and returning with scraped knuckles.

Dammit. Tears well up in his eyes. That sedative was a piece, a major piece, in the plan he conducted for escaping. Sedate a nurse or orderly, steal their key, and escape from the front doors into the dead of night. Without the sedative he has nothing. No leverage. No means. Nothing. Of course, too, now the orderlies would be keeping a closer eye on him. The extent and intensity of their supervision would prevent him from securing another sedative for a while, Hell, he'd probably never get a second chance at having one again.

Dread hangs over his head like a storm cloud as he walks away from the office. With the patients all outside, the interior is unfamiliarly quiet. The halls no longer echo screams and crying but instead reflect the soft pitter-patter of footsteps. He stops at the base of the stairs. The new nurse is a few feet from him. Her back towards him, she is reaching for the doorknob of the slightly opened door to supply closet.

What is she doing? Her presence is a slight distraction from his grief as his curiosity rises.

"It's not safe to wander around all by yourself," he says.

He must have startled the nurse, who jumps up and recoils from the door. Turning to him, Farrah's eyes show uneasiness. Her chest rises and falls quickly as she rests her hand over her heart.

"Jumpy little thing, aren't you?" Nero asks.

He walks towards her.

"I just... wasn't expecting anyone, that's all," she says.

Nero leans in close to the nurse, making her face flush. Her eyes travel from his handsome face to his scarred arms and stop at his bloodied knuckles. Tenderly, she reaches out for his injured hand. He flinches and steps back as soon as her warm fingers touch his skin.

"What happened?"

Nero's eyes avert her gaze, the emotions from the previous event settling back in.

"Nothing, a wall just happened to meet my fist."

She draws her eyebrows together and her lips form a skeptical frown. Without another word the nurse gestures for him to follow her. Intrigued, he lets her lead him to the infirmary.

The infirmary is small, considering most patients are treated in their rooms or during their sessions held in Dr. Chaucer's office. The room is windowless and quite bare. There are two medical beds, equipped with leather straps for a person's arms and legs. Along one wall is a long cabinet which holds a variety of medical items from wraps and gauze to IV equipment and supplies for stitching up an open wound.

Farrah takes a seat on a rolling chair and ushers Nero to sit on the nearest bed. He lies back and positions his arms so that she may strap him down, another habit he's picked up.

"That's not necessary. Please, sit up."

Obedient but confused, Nero does what she asks. Farrah unlocks one of the cabinet's drawers and retrieves rubbing alcohol and some gauze.

"Now, this is going to sting a little," Farrah says.

As promised, the second the stale smelling liquid begins running down his skin it begins to sting. The pain is weak, but it is still comforting. Pain allows him to feel and reminds him that he is still human, no matter what Mark or the other staff members tell him.

"There, all done."

Nero looks down at his hand, which is now bound with white gauze.

"I suggest you refrain from hitting another wall anytime soon, or at least use your other hand when you do," Farrah jokes.

A slight chuckle escapes Nero's lips, surprising them both. He tilts his head to the side, studying Farrah's appearance. His eyes travel up from her thin legs to her face. He is drawn to her big, soft eyes. His cheeks flush and he turns away from her.

"What is it? Do I have something on my face?"

Nero shakes his head. Farrah sighs, scratching the back of her head with her hand. Sheepishly, he looks back at her.

"What is a pretty bird like you doing in such a monstrous place like this?" Nero asks.

"Monstrous? This place helps rehabilitate people and I want to be a part of that process."

Nero releases a howl of maniacal laughter in response to her words. Confusion plagues her face.

"Please tell me how rehabilitating this is."

Nero pushes his hair from his forehead. Both sides of his temples have red circular burns on them. The burnt flesh is uneven with fragments of dead skin loosely attached.

"Oh my God, please don't tell me..." Before she can finish her sentence, Mark runs into the room. His breaths are labored and panicked.

"You were supposed to stay outside the door! I was looking all over for you! You're going into isolation for this," Mark says.

He walks over to Nero, his fists shaking, but Farrah quickly steps in between them.

"He didn't disobey your orders, sir. I...uh I went and retrieved him. I needed help with relocating some medications and after he slipped, I had to come here and bandage his hand."

Nero's eyes widen. Mark's posture loses tension.

"Is this true?" Mark asks.

Farrah turns and looks to Nero, along with Mark.

"Y-yes."

Mark releases a loud sigh and wipes the beaded sweat from his wide forehead. Nero looks up to Farrah, who is focused on the out-of-breath orderly. The air around them is still.

"Do you still need him for help, or can I bring him to join the others?"

"He's all bandaged up and ready to go. Just make sure to go easy on that hand," she says.

The orderly motions for Nero to follow him, who rises in obedience. He hesitates in the doorway, glancing back at Farrah. Her back is already turned to him, putting the medical supplies back in their proper spaces.

As soon as the sunlight meets Nero's face a wave of calm washes over him. He takes refuge under a large oak tree, his usual spot. Two mockingbirds sit atop a low-hanging branch, chirping angrily at one another. Nero closes his eyes. Aside from pain, his only other escape is in his day dreams. Although he has not seen much of the outside world, he imagines it to be beautiful. Large houses filled with books, comfortable beds, and food that actually tastes like food.

"Nero?"

Nero opens one of his eyes. Farrah stands before him. He watches wearily as she sits down a few feet from him.

"When I first got here, I read as many of the patients files as I could. What happened to you... it's inexcusable."

"It's ironic, if anything. In one night, I killed the two monsters who had been haunting me for years," he shakes his head, "yet, here I am, imprisoned, as if I'm the monster."

Farrah places her hand on his shoulder. He flinches and she pulls her hand away.

"Nero, I want to help you."

"Oh, are you going to promise to get me out of here too," he scoffs, "why do you care? I mean really, am I some sort of pet project to you?"

Farrah shakes her head.

"I don't know what I'm going to do, but I've had the same look that you hold in your eyes. I know what it feels like. The feeling of being alone and the emptiness that comes with it."

She rises to her feet and dusts off her skirt.

"Fresh out of college with no experience in an asylum before, it surprised me that I got this job. I don't know what you believe, but I believe in God and divine intervention. There's some reason I ended up here, and I'm starting to believe it was so I could help you."

Unable to respond. Nero watches her as she walks off. He scratches the back of his head. His thoughts are water and her words oil, rising to the top of his mind and unavoidable. *How could she possibly know what I feel like? How could she ever begin to understand?*

The birds are no longer chirping. Nero watches Farrah as she interacts with another patient named Samuel. Samuel is a large Negro man, somewhere in his forties. He is a very angry patient. Only arriving at Winter Grove a few months ago. He still fights protocol and has attempted to escape the facility numerous times, almost as many times as Nero. Samuel was brought in after police officers found him on the street. He was eating a homeless man. Told them he had found the body, but later confessed to kidnapping and eating several other missing people. He swears up and down that cannibalism has kept him looking as young as he does.

Suddenly, Samuel grabs Farrah by her hair and shoves her to the dirt. Nero's eyes widen.

What is he doing? He cannot hear the words being exchanged between the two, but the cross expression on Samuel's face implies he's angry about something. The other nurses are chatting amongst themselves, apparently unmoved by or oblivious to the situation. Curious and confused, Nero rises to his feet, moving towards the large oaf of a man.

Samuel pulls back his fist, making Farrah wince as she prepares for a hit. Nero's brain and body suddenly are on different pages. Before he even realizes what he is doing, he lunges at the patient, knocking him down to the ground. Samuel blurts out some expletives and throws Nero off him. Suddenly his thick brown hands are pounding into Nero's face. Nero thrusts his knee into Samuel's groin, making him lose enough concentration for him to throw Samuel down and exchange places with him. Adrenaline pulses through his veins as his fists pound into Samuel's neck and face. The gauze on his hand reddening with each strike, against the unconscious cannibal.

Nero's ears are deceitful, refusing to pick up any noise besides his own racing pulse. Some orderly grabs his arm, causing him to refocus his offense. His knuckles throb as they meet the orderly's bony neck. He only gets a few blows in before he is knocked backward onto the grass. Jacob holds down his arms, Mark sits on his stomach, and another nurse pricks his neck with a needle. Suddenly his vision blurs, his pulse relaxes, and his body goes limp.

Nero is strapped down to a wooden table when he finally regains consciousness. His head is throbbing, stomach queasy, and his face bruising. The smell of mildew, sweat, and blood engulf him. The air is cold and the room is poorly lit. It could be pitch black and he would still know where he was at. A room like this is too difficult to forget. The sound of footsteps bounces off of the stone walls.

"Glad to see you're awake," Dr. Chaucer says.

Her red hair is pulled back into a ponytail. Mark and a random orderly flank her sides as she approaches Nero. Her wrinkled hands adjust the leather straps on his wrists, practically cutting off the circulation to his hands.

"What you did today was unacceptable. Not only did you engage in physical combat with another patient, but you also injured one of my staff members. Poor George has a black-eye and a possible broken jaw. Do you have anything to say for yourself?" she asks.

Her question is met with silence and a glare from him.

"Well then. I guess there's nothing left to say here. Mark, you may begin. Please return him to his quarters after you're finished. And no dinner for him tonight," she says.

A wicked grin is plastered on Mark's face as the psychiatrist leaves him. The other man slips a mouth-guard in between Nero's lips. It tastes like rubber and sweat. The staff probably never wash it after each treatment. Mark fastens the ECT device on Nero's head, settling the stainless-steel electrodes over his already red temples.

Without prompt or warning, the machine is turned on. Light flashes in Nero's eyes as electricity begins charging through his body. Its loud hum is like the interior of a beehive that has been shaken with fifty angry bees inside. His body convulses uncontrollably as familiar stinging takes over him. The stinging sensation doesn't last long and numbness takes over in its place. His skin under the electrodes begins to peel, releasing the potent odor of burning flesh. Time is an illusion during electric-shock-therapy sessions. Sometimes it feels like an eternity before the waves of electricity dissipate, other times it is over almost instantaneously.

Weak and dazed, Nero is shuffled between the two orderlies back into the facility. His eyes are fixated on the ground and his awkward feet which have forgotten how to walk. Somehow, they manage to drag him up the flight of stairs and through the patient's corridor. Mark shoves him down on the cold, hard ground of his room. Gifting Nero a swift kick to his ribs before leaving him. Silence and darkness swallow him, but do not ease his pain. Tears gracelessly slip down his cheeks, staining his shirt. He pulls his legs to his chest, curling up like an unborn child, and gives in to his fatigue.

The lock on Nero's door clicks, bringing him back from his short rest. Moonlight seeps through the barred window, slightly illuminating the room. A figure slips in from the doorway. Nero cannot tell who it is, temporary blurry vision is one of the side-effects of electric-shock-therapy, so his body tenses up.

"Nero are you okay?"

Nero immediately recognizes the nurse's voice and breathes a sigh of relief. He attempts to sit up but crumbles like a graham cracker. Farrah rushes to his side and helps prop his back against the wall.

"It's a little late for a visit, isn't it?"

"I had to make sure you were ok. None of the other nurses or orderlies would tell me what was happening or where you were. What did they do to you?"

"Nothing they haven't already done to me before."

His eyes are slowly regaining their focus and he is able to see the nurse now. The moon's beams are highlighting her cheekbones. Her eyes reflect compassion, something unfamiliar to him.

Nero manipulates his shaking hand into raising the hair from his forehead. His temples have new blisters and are bloody. Farrah's fingers delicately trace the circumference of the scars, tears welling up in her eyes.

"I'm so sorry, this is all my fault. I wasn't paying attention to where I was walking and ran right into the back of Samuel. And then I said the wrong thing and it just escalated from there."

Her shoulders hunch forward, shaking gently as tears fall down her cheeks. Nero brings his hand to her chin, awkwardly lifting her face so their eyes are level.

"Look, don't burden yourself with this. They were already going to punish me for stealing a sedative. Protecting you just g-gave them a reason to get it over with."

Nero's expression changes to embarrassment and shock as he realizes what he just said.

Was I really protecting her? Before his mind can even begin to process the idea, Farrah wraps her arms around his waist and pulls him into a tight embrace. Her wet face presses against his chest. Nero's face flushes. He doesn't know what to do. Half of his mind is telling him to push her away, the other half is wanting to comfort her.

Nero raises his arms, levitating them awkwardly above her. Farrah's sniffling has stopped, and the world around them is silent minus their rapidly beating hearts. Nero surrenders, letting his arms weave around her and resting his head against her peach-scented hair. A strange feeling is budding in his stomach. For the first time since stepping foot inside Winter Grove, he doesn't wish he is anywhere else.

Mercy was first published in Mercy: A Short Story Collection in March 2019.

6

Rookie Mistake

It's a cool October evening. The full moon rests on top of wispy clouds. The Cat Club bar is unusually quiet for a Monday night. Dorian sits at the bar. His pale hand rocks a half-empty glass of Pendleton. The ice cubes quietly clink against the glass. His long blonde hair is pulled into a messy braid. He sighs.

"Mr. Blackwell?"

His dry eyes turn from the glass. In front of him is a small, college-aged girl. Thick black frame glasses sit atop her nose. Her wavy chocolate colored hair rests atop her shoulders. She's dressed in a pumpkin orange colored shirt with a navy-blue skirt. He cocks an eyebrow.

"Do I know you?" he asks.

"Mr. Blackwell, it's me, Paige. I'm in Dr. Stern's six o'clock intermediate art history class on Tuesdays and Thursdays, I sit in the front," she says.

Of course, *Paige*, how could he ever forget her? Every class day, without fail, she's early, and every day she's always the last to leave. Always the last to turn in papers, always the most to ask questions, she lingers. Her *Victoria's Secret* perfume is strong enough that it can be smelled from the classroom across the hall. Her heart rate increases every time she's within five feet of him, and every time he glances in her direction.

"Right, Paige, I'm sorry, I'm just not used to seeing students outside of class."

She smiles. "No worries. Mind if I sit?"

"Go ahead."

She takes a seat at the empty bar stool next to him. Her perfume is overshadowed by the strong scent of tequila. She's been drinking to the point that her blood would be sour, unlike the typical sweetness of O positive.

"Can I get a Mojito, please," she turns towards Dorian, "what are you doing in a bar this far out of town?"

He takes a sip of his whiskey. "I could be asking you the same question. I live nearby."

"Oh. I was actually on a date or supposed to be anyway."

That would explain the tequila. "What happened?"

"He stood me up."

Dorian grits his teeth. *I shouldn't have asked.* She toys with the straw in the Mojito.

"It's fine, it's not a big deal or anything," she gulps down her drink, "it's not like I drove forty minutes or anything... Bartender, can I get another please?"

Dorian shakes his head at the bartender. "I think you've had enough."

"Don't be such a spoil sport."

"Paige, I'm serious. I think you need to sober up so you can drive home."

She rolls her eyes. "I can just drive now, it's not a big deal."

She tries to take a step but stumbles and nearly falls. Dorian grabs her wrist. The warmth of her skin sends a shiver up his spine.

"Just take a seat and…"

Paige throws up. The vomit encompasses the floor and stains her shoes.

"Seriously dude?" the bartender says.

Dorian apologizes, tossing enough cash to cover his tab and then some, and drags Paige outside of the bar. Goosebumps cover Paige's tanned skin. Embarrassed, she refuses to make eye contact. Dorian takes his jacket off and wraps it around her shoulders.

"I'm sorry."

"It's alright. Come on, let's get you somewhere warm where you can sober up."

"Where?"

Dorian scratches the back of his head. "I guess we can go to my place. As long as you promise not to mention this to anyone, ever. It would look bad and could put my job in jeopardy."

Her eyes light up. "I would *never* think of doing that."

The ten-minute car ride back to his house feels like an hour. She wouldn't stop talking. Dorian is able to tune her out, for the most part. He only offers an occasional nod or "uh-huh" to make her think he is listening.

Dorian rents a small house where the nearby lots house vacant, dilapidated houses. The grass and weeds are overgrowing in his front lawn. Most of the bushes in his flowerbed are dead, but the ones still alive are misshapen and poor. Several of the screens are torn from the windows, lying against the red brick. The only illumination is provided by a flickering porch lamp.

"This...is charming," she says.

Dorian shrugs his shoulders. He unlocks the front door and escorts her inside. The living room is small, and unorganized. Books upon books are scattered about the floor, coffee table, and couch, as well as overpacked on the shelves. A cat tree is slid against the bay window, where a black Sphynx is dozing.

"Oh he's... cute?"

Paige extends her hand to the cat, awkwardly padding its oily skin. It curls back its lips and hisses. She barely has enough time to recoil her hand, narrowly missing a bite.

"Don't mind Ramses, he's not a fan of humans," he moves a pile of books from the L-shaped couch onto the floor, "why don't you remove your shoes and have a seat?"

She tosses her foul-smelling shoes outside the door and sits on the couch. Dorian goes to the kitchen and returns with two glasses, wine for him and water for her. He takes a seat on the couch away from her, giving a few feet of distance.

"You don't have to sit so far away," she takes a sip of the water, "I won't bite."

Dorian nearly spits out his wine.

"Um, that's ok. You're just here to get sober, remember?"

She sets the glass down and scoots towards him. "I don't have to be."

Her hand traces the seams of his jean pocket before sliding towards his groin. He jumps back.

"Paige, stop."

"Why? We're two adults. What's the harm in having a little fun?"

He shakes his head adamantly. "I'm not interested."

She frowns, pulling her hand back into her lap. A few awkward minutes of silence pass by. Paige is texting and scrolling through her phone. Dorian doesn't know what to say. *Just a few more minutes, she'll surely be sober enough to drive by the time I take her back to her car... right?*

Suddenly, Paige is sitting against him. She fingers his neck, making his entire body tense up. His stomach growls.

"Please stop." He pushes her hand away.

"Come on, Mr. Blackwell, one kiss won't hurt."

"You don't understand, I can't..."

She pulls herself into his lap. Cold sweat beads on his entire body. Saliva is building in his mouth. Paige leans in close to his face, teasingly brushing her lips against his. His trembling hand caresses the back of her head before grabbing a handful of hair and pulling her face to the side of his. His icy lips press against her cheek and slowly travel down to her neck. Gently he kisses her neck, making her melt into his grasp, before softly biting her skin.

Almost like a switch being flipped, his gentle actions transform to brutal. Paige lets out a blood curdling scream as his fangs pierce through her flesh and sink into her jugular. Crimson fluid gushes from her punctured skin onto the wild-eyed vampire and seeps through his cotton shirt. Dorian's body starts shaking violently as he begins drinking her blood. Despite the alcohol, the taste is still sweet and orgasmic.

"Why...what are you..."

She tries to pull away, but her body is frozen. Dorian's grip is too strong. She opens her mouth to scream again, but no sound comes out. Tears stroll down her cheeks as the color fades from her face. Her eyes are dulling as rapidly as her pulse. Paige's body goes limp as Dorian takes one final slurp. He pushes her arms away from him, the force knocking her off the couch and onto the shag carpeting. He wipes the excess blood from his face and licks it off his fingers. Ramses meows, his yellow eyes fixated on Dorian.

"What?"

The sphynx stares blankly at him. He sighs.

"If only cats could talk," he looks down at Paige's body, "on second thought, it's probably best they don't."

The next evening, Dorian went to class as per usual. The instructor, seeing Paige's empty chair, simply marked her absent and then cruised right on through the lecture. Class ends early, a quiz finishing off the hour. As Dorian is gathering up papers, a chubby girl approaches him. He waits for her to hand him a paper, but she isn't holding anything.

"I guess you two had a long night," she says, winking.

Dorian looks at the girl, tilting his head slightly.

"Pardon me? What are you talking about?"

"No need to be coy. I am Jessica, you know, Paige's roommate. I know all about your late-night rendezvous. She texted me and said she was probably going to be out all night."

Dorian's cold, dead heart falls to his stomach as he processes her words. He could already see his future. Police officers banging on his door, missing posters featuring Paige's most recent selfie, and news reporters sharing his image across the nation.

"Don't worry, Mr. Blackwell, I'm not going to tell the professor. Just make sure you tell Paige she needs to come home tonight so we can study for our Chemistry test tomorrow," she pauses, studying his appearance, "are you ok? You look pale...Or I guess I should say paler than usual."

Rookie Mistake was first published in Mercy: A Short Story Collection in March 2019.

7

Past Discretion

The only noise that can be heard in the hotel room is the humming of the air-conditioning vent as it strains to blow out cool air. Rebecca stands at the kitchenette, twirling a glass half-filled with Jameson. Her delicate face, painted with powder and pink blush, is pained. Her blonde brow is furrowed as she stares at the glass. Adam sits at the edge of the bed. His long legs are crossed. His chocolate brown hair, messy and untamed, covers his forehead. A smug look sets on his face.

"I didn't expect you to be here," Rebecca says.

She takes a drink from the glass. Her lips purse in distaste as the whiskey burns her tongue.

"It is quite the coincidence. You, a bridesmaid in *my* cousin's wedding." he says.

Rebecca takes her glass to the window. Walking past him, she doesn't even offer a sideways glance. The curtains are parted, inviting the lights of the Las Vegas strip into the dimly lit room. She winces as she forces herself to take another sip.

"Why are you drinking that? I seem to recall, you hated whiskey," he says.

Rebecca shrugs her shoulders.

"I'm surprised you would even remember that. How long has it been? Five years?" she says.

Adam chuckles. "Three, it's been three, Becky."

"Don't call me that."

Adam stands up. He glides over to her. She shudders as his hands grope her forearms.

"Didn't you miss me, Becky?"

His hot breath presses against her neck. She tries to wriggle out from his grasp, but his grip tightens, tearing the sleeve on her dress.

"Let me go."

"Why? You used to not mind my company," his right hand slides to her breast, "Actually, you rather *enjoyed* it."

She stomps her heel into his black dress boot. He stumbles back. She flips around, throwing the whiskey glass at him. It barely misses his head, but his hair is now soaked. He shakes his head, laughing maniacally.

"I don't remember you being so feisty."

Suddenly, he lunges. He pins her against the window. His right hand restrains her wrists, while his left arm is pressed against her neck.

She swallows the lump in her throat. "My boyfriend is downstairs at the reception. He's probably looking for me right now."

Adam leans in close to her face.

"Oh, that scrawny guy you were dancing with? Does he know what you do for a living?"

"Leave him out of this, my personal life is none of your business."

He applies more pressure to her neck, making her cough.

"Now, is that any way to talk to one of your best *clients*?"

"Former client." She coughs again. "I don't do that any-more."

"But you were so good at it."

He alleviates some of the pressure on her neck. His chapped lips press against hers, gagging her with kisses. The nightmarish memories she'd worked so hard to repress, come flooding back; the seedy motels, random men, and the sex smell, that no matter how many times she bathed, would never wash away. It wasn't something she had wanted to do, but she had no choice. Struggling to find a job after gradu-ation, drowning in her student loan debt, she had no other choice, or at least that's what she tells herself, to make it easier to sleep at night.

With all her strength, she bites down on his tongue. Warm blood seeps from his mouth into hers. He jerks back, shriek-ing as he falls to his knees. Rebecca rushes to the closet. Prying the sliding door open, she claws at the top of the shelf, and retrieves a small, black handgun. Adam is on his feet, blood oozes from his lips.

"You bitch."

His eyes widen as she steadies the gun, aiming it at his chest. He holds his hands in the air.

"Easy there, Becky, put the gun down."

"Shut the fuck up." She cocks the gun. "I need you listen carefully, I'm only going to say this once."

Unable to hide his uneasiness, he nods.

"First off, you're going to get out of my room. You're going to get your things from your room, promptly check out, and leave the hotel. You're going to get in whatever piece of shit car you drove here, drive to the airport, and go back to wherever the fuck you came from. My face? You're going to forget it. My name? Keep it out of your mouth."

"I need to say goodbye to my cousin before I go."

She shakes her head. "Were you not listening to me?"

"I heard you, but..."

"Then get the hell out of here!"

Taking several large, but quick steps, he heads for the door. Hand on the knob, he lingers as if he's going to say something, but he doesn't. As soon as the door closes, Rebecca locks it. She slides down into a crumpled heap on the floor. Her heart feels like it's going to jump out of her chest. She opens the chamber of the gun. It's empty. Rebecca jumps as the doorknob is jerked, followed by a knock on the door.

"Hey babe are you ok?" a voice calls out.

Rebecca sighs, relieved. "Yeah, hang on a second."

She hides the gun back in the closet. Wiping the mascara from underneath her eyes, she goes to the door. Her hands are still shaky, but she opens it anyway. She practically jumps in her boyfriend's arms, knocking him back a few steps.

"Hey, what's wrong, are you alright?"

She buries her face in his chest, inhaling his sweet cologne.

"I'm fine... I just saw someone I used to know, that's all."

Past Discretion was first published in Mercy: A Short Story Collection in March 2019.

8

It Could be Worse

"That cute red-head left you a number on the receipt," Mitch says.

Jay looks up from the table he's clearing. "Really?"

It's almost three o' clock in the afternoon. The last customer has just walked out of Starlight Café, and the staff is going through the daily closing routine. The Starlight Café is a quiet, country-inspired restaurant. Metal yard art animals, including chickens and pigs, are strategically placed around the interior. Red faux leather is the base and back for the booths and the chair's interior lining. The staff all wear jeans, button down shirts, and bandannas. One of the waiters, Jay, is a twenty-one-year old college student studying criminal psychology at the local university. He is tall and thin. Curly blonde hair frames his boyish face.

Jay looks at the receipt. His green eyes widen. Not only is a phone number scribbled at the bottom, but the girl left a fifty-dollar tip for an eight-dollar meal. He pulls out his iPhone and snaps a picture of the receipt.

"Are you going to text her?" Mitch asks.

Mitch, who is also twenty-one, is Jay's closest friend and roommate. He had gotten Jay the job at Starlight Café. He's short and a little heavy sat. A journalism major, he usually has a pencil perched behind his ear and a notepad nearby, in case something newsworthy occurs.

Jay shrugs his shoulders. "I don't know, I just broke up with Sasha not too long ago..."

"If I remember correctly, Sasha broke up with YOU after she admitted she was seeing someone else."

"Thanks for the reminder."

"Look, all I'm saying is it could do you some good to get some female attention," he puts his hand on Jay's shoulder, "besides, if it doesn't work out, you could always introduce her to your better-looking co-worker."

Jay rolls his eyes. They both laugh.

Jay sits in a coffee shop. Across from him sits a beautiful girl. Her fiery red hair is pulled into a messy brain. She's wearing a tight, black dress with a grey cardigan over it.

"I'm so glad you texted me," Eve says.

"Yeah, thanks for agreeing to meet up," he takes a sip of his black coffee, "why don't you tell me about yourself?"

"Well, I'm currently taking a break from college, but I'm a fashion design major. I work at Daisy's Boutique on the square."

"Why are you taking a break?"

Her smile fades. "Personal reasons."

"Sorry, I didn't mean to intrude."

"It's alright, I'll forgive you, *this time*," the smile returns to her face, "I have the cutest little dog."

Before he can respond, she pulls out her phone. She shoves the phone close to Jay's face. Her lock screen is a giant, steel grey Pitbull. The dog is fashioned in a black spike collar.

"Oh wow. He's cute, but I'm more of a cat person. I have a Siamese, and my roommate Mitch has an orange tabby."

Eve pulls her phone back. "*She*. My Miley could kill a cat with one bite."

He laughs nervously.

"I'm not kidding."

He opens his mouth to say something but doesn't. A few awkward, long seconds pass by. The round clock on the wall reads ten o'clock. He'd only been on this date for fifteen minutes, but he was ready to call it a quits. *Say you have to go. Could try faking a seizure... just tell her it isn't working out, something....*

"What about you?" she asks.

"Um, I'm a criminal psychology major. I'm hoping to graduate next summer."

She scoffs. "That's a stupid major. What can you even do with that degree?"

"Well someday I would like to be a detective." He stands up. "Please excuse me for a moment."

Jay rushes to the men's bathroom. He pulls out his phone, opening a text conversation with Mitch.

"Please come rescue me. This is the WORST date I've ever been on. I'm at the coffee shop on 2nd Avenue, next to the guitar store," he texts.

He takes a deep breath before exiting the restroom. If he hadn't left his coat at the table, he could've just walked out. *I could always buy another coat with the fifty dollars she gave me...*

"Jay? What're you doing just standing there?" Eve calls out.

"Sorry, I, uh." He begrudgingly sits back down, "Spaced out for a sec."

Jay's phone pings. He immediately pulls it out. A text from Mitch reads, "You'll owe me BIG TIME for this. Be there in a few."

He sighs.

Eve snaps her fingers at him. "Excuse me?"

He looks up from his phone.

"Can you possibly be ruder than you're being right now? Texting on a date, where's your manners?"

He slides his phone back into his pocket. "Sorry."

"So, where are we going to go after this? I was thinking we could play it safe with a movie, but if you really want to, we could go back to my place and *hangout*."

A shiver runs up his spine. "What movie did you have in mind?"

"Well, we could go see that new rom-com with Rebel Wilson, all my girlfriends say it's amazing."

"Why don't you see what the showtimes for it are?" he asks.

"Ok."

She pulls out her phone. Jay glances at the clock. It's only 10:18 a.m. *Come on, Mitch. You have to hurry.* He nervously strums his fingers on the table,

"So, there's a showing at eleven, one-thirty, four.... five-thirty, and seven-forty-five."

The bell over the door rings. Somewhat out-of-breath, Mitch walks over to the table.

"Oh my God, Jay, I've been looking everywhere for you," he says.

"Why? Is something wrong?" Jay asks.

"Your cat threw up all over the place. It's on the rug, the carpet, my shoes," he looks down at his feet, "not these shoes, my other ones."

Jay forces his best concerned expression on his face. "Oh no, that's not good at all."

"Yeah, you better get home, right away. She needs to go to a vet."

"You're probably right."

He stands up and swiftly puts on his coat.

A cross expression is on Eve's face. "Wait a minute."

The guys look at each other nervously.

"We're on a date right now. Can't this wait?"

"No," they both say in unison.

She pouts. "Fine, go. We can see the movie another time."

"Definitely."

Jay didn't reply to the texts she sent the day of their date or the two days following. After receiving countless phone calls and cringeworthy voicemails, he blocked her number. He ignored her *Facebook* friend request and didn't follow her back on *Twitter* or *Instagram*. He assumed she would get the message.

Jay is tired. Puffy bags sit under his eyes. His body clock always takes some time to adjust after a few days off and the four-a.m. wake-up call was not pleasant this morning. It's almost six o' clock, and the staff is preparing to open the café. Jay puts on his black apron, sticking several dozen straws in its side pocket.

"Hey, Jay," Mitch comes around from the kitchen, "got a second?"

"Yeah. What's up?"

Mitch leads him to a booth in the far corner, away from the prying ears of their co-workers.

"You know Kaylee, the new hostess?"

Jay nods.

"Well I was talking to her this morning and she said Eve has been here the past two days asking to be sat in your section," he lowers his voice, "she also said that Eve gets more than a little upset whenever she finds out you're not here."

"You have got to be kidding me..."

"Kaylee hasn't said anything to anyone else, but she said if she does it again, she's going to *have* to tell one of the managers."

"Great, I'm going to lose my job because some whack job."

"It could be worse. She could be ugly," Mitch jokes.

Jay groans and puts his face in his hands.

"Alright guys, time to look alive. Doors are opening, be ready," the manager calls out.

Mitch puts his hand on Jay's shoulder before walking to the front. Jay doesn't move. Low murmurs echo off the wood paneled wall as the crowd slowly shuffles into the café. *Everything will be fine. If she shows up, I'll just talk to her.* He forces himself to stand up.

Three hours into his shift and there's no sign of Eve. He's been making good tips and indulging in enough conversation that he had almost forgotten about her. Almost.

"Can I take my break?" Jay asks.

The manager checks his watch. He's an older male, somewhere in his fifties, with a passion for business and the café; however, he isn't the best at managing. More times than not, he refuses to give the wait staff any breaks and is quick to lose his temper when there's a problem.

"After you take the drink order from the person Kaylee just sat in your section, you can."

Jay walks to the small table, normally seated for two. He pulled out his little notebook and pen, flipping it to a blank page.

"Good morning, my name is Jay and I'll be your server today. What can I get you started for a drink?"

"I know who you are."

He looks up and his stomach drops to the floor. Eve is sitting alone at the table. An ugly scowl is plastered on her face.

"Hi Eve. I didn't realize you were here."

She scoffs. "Oh, so you weren't able to run and hide like the past two days when I showed up?"

"I was off."

Out of the corner of his eye, Jay sees his manager staring at him. *Is he listening? Can he feel the tension?*

"What would you like to drink?" he asks again.

"Why haven't you texted me back?"

Jay nervously wipes the sweat from his forehead.

"Eve, this is not the time or the place to talk about this, I'm working right now. Maybe after my shift we can talk."

"NO," she slams her fist on the table, rattling the silverware, "I want to know NOW."

Jay bites his lip. Suddenly, his manager is standing next to him.

"Is everything alright over here?" the manager asks.

Eve bursts into tears. "H-he told m-m-e I'm not w-w-welcome here."

Jay's mouth falls open. "That's not true! She's lying, trying to get me in trouble!"

Her crying intensifies.

"W-why w-w-would I lie?"

Jay opens his mouth to speak but can't. His manager gives him a sharp glare, something of the choose-your-next-words-carefully kind of glares. He waves Mitch over to the table. Mitch and Jay exchange uncomfortable glances.

"This is Mitch. He will be your server today. I promise you, I will handle this. I apologize on his behalf, please know this kind of behavior is not acceptable. And for your troubles, your meal is on the house today."

Roughly, the manager grabs Jay's arm and practically drags him into the break area. His round face is red. Anger seeps out of his over-sized pores.

"What the hell was that?"

"I can explain! She's a crazy girl that I went out on a date with a few days ago. I didn't respond to her texts and now she's pissed."

"Kaylee told me this is the third day she's been here," he shakes his head, "do you know how this looks for business?"

Jay fidgets with the hem of his apron.

"Bad?"

"VERY bad."

"Sir, listen...."

"No, no more talking. Go hang up your apron."

Jay's face drops. "What? Why? Am I fired?"

"I don't know yet. I'm going to take you off the schedule for the next two weeks. If she stops showing up, I'll give you a call. If you don't hear from me, then you have your answer."

"Please don't do this," Jay fights back tears, "I have rent coming up, payment for fall tuition, groceries. I *need* this job."

His manager shakes his head. "I'm not going to argue with you, kid. Get out of here."

Jay sits on the floor in his apartment bedroom with his laptop in his lap. A Siamese cat is nestled in a ball beside him. He can't concentrate on his homework. He opens a tab and goes to *Facebook*. The only notification is for Eve's unanswered friend request. He clicks on her profile. Her privacy settings are low and most of her posts are visible. She's posted hundreds of selfies, all with either an inspirational quote or a popular song lyric as the caption. There's also an absurd amount of dog pictures. Scrolling through, a comment on one of her posts catches his attention.

It reads, "Sorry to hear you were kicked out of school baby girl. Don't worry, this will all figure itself out. Stay strong. xoxoxo"

Intrigued, Jay opens another tab. He types her full name. Over two hundred matches with her name pop up in *Google*.

'Girl kicked out of university for stalking star athlete; Violated restraining order again and again; In police custody; Not the first time; Allegedly keyed victim's car, slashed tires, and poisoned dog; Injuries ending athlete's career; Made bail; Psychiatric evaluation underway; Public apology; Light sentencing, more like a slap on the wrist; Sentence reduced due to good behavior; Victim forced to relocate.'

The color drains from Jay's face. His stomach churns. If he had eaten earlier, he probably would've thrown up. Suddenly, his phone rings. Jay scrambles to grab it from off the bed. It's Mitch calling. *Why is he calling? He shouldn't be done until four, half past three at the earliest...*

"Hey Mitch, what's going on?" he answers.

"Hello Jay. Are you ready to talk now?" Eve says.

He drops the phone. It falls to the ground with a low thud.

It Could be Worse was first published in Mercy: A Short Story Collection in March 2019.

9

Blood Snow

It is a frigid Winter morning. The moon has just retired, and the sun is fighting to break through the thick clouds. Snow, at least three feet high in most places, covers the landscape of Breyerdale. A lone man, a farmer in his late twenties, rides through the bland, endless sea of white. The only contrasting color are the bare trees, colored in burnt umber hues, that line his path. His mount, a pale grey Andalusian with a steel grey mane and tail, is damp with sweat. The mare's nostrils are flaring as she breathes in the icy air.

"Easy girl," he says.

The horse slows down to a quick trot. The air around them is quiet, minus birds chirping in the distance and the faint sound of a nearby river. Snow crunches beneath the horse's hooves with each step she takes. The man draws back his hood, revealing his brown curls and young face. Uneasiness lingers in his eyes.

Should I rest or is it too soon? His body aches with the wind's chill. Fashioned only in an old shirt, worn trousers and green hooded cloak, his clothes are moist from the heavy flurries. His nose is red, and a thin layer of snot rests atop his lip. Hours earlier, he had stripped all evidence tying him to King Brevern's army and slipped away from the battlefield during the dead of night. No more armor to protect him, no shield, and only the sword he inherited from his father to protect him now. The mare snorts and blood and mucus spew from her nostrils. He knows he had pushed the horse too hard, but he had no choice.

Only two days prior, he had received a letter. His wife had passed away of a mysterious and sudden illness, leaving his young son, Barlow, alone. His neighbor, who had written the letter, offered to house the boy, but she was elderly and stressed that she could only watch after him for a brief period of time.

A twig snaps behind him, and a cold shiver runs up the man's spine. He aggressively kicks his heels into the animal's sides. The horse doesn't pick up its pace, instead it plants its hooves firmly. He kicks it again, but the horse refuses to move. Heart racing, he quickly dismounts and rushes forward. There's the sound of a stray horse stomping through snow. It grows closer and closer until it sounds like it's going to run him over.

"Elijah is that you?" a voice calls out.

Suddenly, a man on horseback is blocking his path. The man is in his mid-thirties. His long black hair and dark beard match the mood of the war. His wrinkled forehead and the wide scar across his cheek reflect the hardships of his life.

Fallon? Elijah stops. His trembling hand grips the handle of his sword. With labored breaths, and numb legs, he struggles not to collapse. Fallon was a blacksmith prior to the war with Voltaire. He too was drafted unwillingly and forced into the cavalry. Elijah had fought in several battles alongside Fallon. Fallon had even shared rabbit and other game his falcon had caught with Elijah after the rations had become scarce. Without Fallon, Elijah would have endured multiple days without food, much like the other members of the cavalry and infantry. Not only did Fallon provide meals, he also provided companionship for the young farmer. A father himself, Fallon seemed to empathize with Elijah's struggle of being away from his son.

"I saw you leave last night. I tried to catch up with you as quickly as I could, but my horse clearly is no match for yours," Fallon says.

Fallon dismounts his horse. He is still wearing Breyerdale armor. Even his horse, a stout bay stallion, wears a saddle pad with the kingdom's emblem, a lion with a snake in between its teeth. Elijah takes a step back, his grip tightening around his sword's handle. Fallon takes a step forward, pushing Elijah to take another step back.

"Are you feeling alright, friend?" Fallon asks.

Elijah looks around. There doesn't appear to be anyone else, but why would Fallon still be wearing the kingdom's armor? Sure, Fallon had talked about deserting, as most men had. With Voltaire's army securing multiple victories in the prominent northern outposts, they had good reason to worry. Every victory brought the enemy closer, and it was only a matter of time before the western outposts were hit. A handful of soldiers had starved to death and more than a dozen men had already attempted to desert the posts, but they were always caught and publicly executed.

"Please, let me go. Barlow is only four," tears well up in his eyes, "Mary is dead. He has no one."

"Easy there," Fallon drops his sheathed sword to the ground and raises his hands defensively, "I'm not going to hurt you."

Elijah draws his sword. He pictures Barlow; his big blue eyes, curly brown hair, and freckled face. His nose, petite and slightly curved, resembles that of his mother's. According to the letter, the child had found his mother, unmoving and cold. lying in the bed. He had been too scared to leave the modest farm house. Three days passed before the elderly woman had come over and found the sniveling boy along with his dead mother. Three days without food, human contact, or sleep.

"Please, let me take your horse. I need to go home"

He smiles meekly. "I'm afraid I can't let you do that."

Using the remainder of his strength, Elijah rushes at Fallon. He drives his sword at Fallon's chest, in attempt to push him back. Fallon reaches for his sword on the ground, but Elijah defers him, slicing into his hand and making him stumble back. Running past him, Elijah grabs a lock of the stallion's thick mane and pulls himself into the saddle. His sword falls to the ground as the horse breaks into a gallop.

A sharp pain suddenly pierces Elijah's shoulder as an arrow breaks through his coat and meets his muscle. Before he can even think, another arrow whizzes into his thigh. A third arrow hits the horse's right hock. The horse stumbles, and crashes into the snow, pinning Elijah's leg underneath it. Elijah tries to move, but he's stuck. He feels numb, the adrenaline, shock, and freezing cold are enough to mask his pain.

Fallon walks up, holding his sword in his injured hand. He presses the blade through the horse's temple. Immediately it stops struggling. He looks at Elijah. His brown eyes are empty, vacant of any emotion.

"Why?" Elijah asks.

Fallon puts the tip of his sword against Elijah's angular jawline. Several members from the king's army ride up and form a circle around the two men. Their expressions are as cold as the snow beneath their horse's hooves.

"You deserted your post and abandoned your king. For what reason? Oh, the rations are low, war is *hard*, I miss my family," he says.

Elijah shakes his head, enabling the blade to tear into his pale skin. Crimson blood slips down his neck and into the snow, reddening it.

"I left for my son... he needs me. Fallon, please don't do this," he coughs, "all I was trying to do was get home to him."

Fallon crouches down in the snow next to him. The numbness is now gone, replaced by a constant throbbing throughout his entire body.

"We all have families, those of us who have fallen and those of us who are still left to fight. You aren't special," he says.

"I thought... you'd understand. I thought...."

"You thought what? We were friends or something? You were nothing more than a temporary ally."

Elijah opens his mouth to speak but can't. He reaches for the letter in his cloak pocket, but he is too weak to grasp it. If only Fallon would read it, maybe, just maybe, he would show mercy.

"You're a coward. Running away, makes you just as bad as the scoundrels in Voltaire's army."

Fallon rises to his feet. Slowly he relinquishes the sword into Elijah's neck, his body contorts from the pain. Blood flows heavily from the gash. As more blood evacuates his body his breaths grow shallow. The clouds have completely over-taken the sun and a cold, heavy rain starts. Droplets pitter-patter against the snow, drowning out the noise of the king's men as they retreat. Fallon lingers, watching his former comrade as he slowly fades from consciousness.

Blood Snow was first published in Mercy: A Short Story Collection in March 2019.

10 |

Unexpected Loss

Something didn't feel right. The voicemail left by the vet tech is vague, but Shawn knows something bad had happened. As soon as he listened to it, he took off from work. There is no way he would be able to focus on his customers or their tax issues, with the weight of uncertainty that the message gave him. It was just supposed to be a routine teeth cleaning for his dog, Ellie. The little tan and white rat terrier is old, almost thirteen years old; however, besides the plaque growing on her teeth, her only signs of aging are the cloudiness forming in her eyes and the extra white hairs overtaking the brown on her head.

Shawn sits in the back office at the veterinary clinic. Its walls are white, and the floor is a pale pink tile. There's a poster on the wall with a cat and dog, advertising some expensive flea and tick product. A clear bin, holding several old *Catster* magazines is also mounted on the wall. He runs his hand through his curly brown hair. He can't help but tap his black soled sneaker against the floor, a nervous habit he can't seem to shake. Suddenly there's a tap on the door. The vet tech, a tall and lanky boy who's only several years younger than Shawn, and the vet, a woman in her early forties, enter the room.

The tech's fingers are wrapped around Ellie's chart. Twelve years of information regarding the dog's health and medications, are secured on the clipboard. Perhaps even the information regarding the day's procedure are mixed in. The tech's eyes are focused on the floor, refusing to even look in Shawn's direction. He normally never shuts up. Something's not right.

"Good afternoon Shawn. How are you?" the vet asks.

Shawn shrugs his shoulders. "Could be better, I didn't really understand the message you guys left me. Did Ellie's procedure go okay?"

The vet takes a deep breath. Shawn bites his chapped lip.

"I'm sorry to tell you this Shawn, but Ellie passed away."

Shawn was only thirteen when he got Ellie. He had begged his parents for a dog for years until they finally caved. Out of all of the dogs and cats at the animal shelter, he was drawn to the wiry haired dog. Barely a year old, the terrier had already been through a lot. Her original owners had neglected and abused her. When he first brought her home, she was afraid of everything and everyone. The simple beeping of a microwave was enough to send her running to another room. Through months of patience and love, Ellie had learned to trust Shawn and they had grown a formidable bond.

"What do you mean she passed?"

"Everything was going great, we had finished scraping her teeth and were in the process of bringing her out of anesthesia," the vet takes a deep breath, "but she didn't wake up. We tried to resuscitate her, but in the end, we weren't able to. I'm so sorry Shawn."

Shawn feels numb. He doesn't know what to say. All he wants to do is cry. Ellie has always been there for him. She was there when he told his parents he was gay, went through his first big breakup, and after his suicide attempt. Ellie is, or *was*, his world.

"Would you like to see her?" she asks.

"Yes."

The vet left the room. Shawn couldn't hold in the tears anymore. Effortlessly, they slid down his cheeks. The vet tech awkwardly stood in the room, not saying anything. Even if he had spoken, it would not have made Shawn feel any better. It felt like an eternity before the veterinarian returned. In her arms, wrapped in a pale pink towel, is Ellie.

"Can I hold her?" he asked.

Without a word, the vet carefully places the dog into his arms. Trembling, Shawn cradles her lifeless body. Her little eyes are closed, and her tongue is protruding from between her lips. If he didn't know any better, he would think she is asleep. He lowers his head, burying his snot covered lip into the dog's stiff hair.

"We'll give you a few minutes alone, don't hesitate to let us know if you need anything."

He didn't hear the vet, or the tech leave the room, but loneliness sweeps in as soon as the door is closed. He had never felt lonely with Ellie around before, but it doesn't feel like her anymore. Sure, it's her body, but everything that made her the dog she was, her soul, is gone. He strokes her wiry hair.

Her body is limp and cold. Looking at her is hard, but he forces himself to. This is the last day he will ever see his dog. Sure, he'll always have the pictures and the happy memories, but nothing compares the real thing. Nothing will ever be the same again.

Unexpected Loss was first published in Mercy: A Short Story Collection in March 2019.

11 |

Guilty by Association

It was an early December morning and the stars shimmered bright against the Texas sky. The roads were treated in preparation for the upcoming snow storm, but the cars were few and far between. It was as if the potential threat of bad weather had everyone at home, bunkered down. Rob and his two teenage friends stood on the vacant highway overpass. They were all warmly dressed in winter coats, knitted hats, and pants. A large bucket of rocks sat by their feet. The chilly air nipped at their finger-tips.

"We picked the worst night to do this," Nathaniel sighed.

"Just be patient," Doug said. He was the shortest and stoutest of the two friends as well as the ringleader of the group. His gaze was fixated on the stretch of road ahead of them, as if he could will some sorry sucker to drive through.

Rob was quiet. His hands were shoved in his pockets to hide their nervous trembling. Part of him hoped no one would be out on the road, and that Doug's stupid idea would be forgotten as easily as their assignments before winter break. Doug said it would be a fun prank, but it seemed more dangerous and reckless than anything else. Rob's posture stiffened as a pair of headlights appeared in the distance.

"This is it boys," Doug feverishly rubbed his hands together. "It's time to assume our positions."

Nathaniel grinned as he grabbed the left side of the bucket while Doug grabbed the right. They both grunted as they struggled to lift it over the concrete wall. The closer the vehicle got, the queasier Rob felt. He could try and stop them, sure, but it's not like it would prevent them from trying again on the next passing car. He knew his friends, and once they decided to do something, they wouldn't stop trying until it was done.

"Get over here and help," Doug said.

Rob tried to move, but it was like his boots were glued to the ground. Doug said something on the lines of, "Stop being a pussy," but Rob didn't hear him. He only heard his own heart racing. Nathaniel and Doug managed to sling the bucket over the edge right as the vehicle, a dark-colored pickup truck, had reached the shadow of the overpass. Everything felt like it was happening in slow motion. The truck swerved as the rocks bounced off the hood and smashed through the windshield. It shot across the other lane and collided into the concrete medium. Doug and Nathaniel appeared to be in shock or awe, motionless as smoke erupted from the stationary truck.

"What did you two idiots just do?" Rob asked.

They didn't respond. Rob attempted to take a step towards them, but they were already running in the opposite direction towards the nearby woods. Rob flipped around and high-tailed it after them. Dense brush, and fallen branches snagged at all three of the teenagers as they ran. Rob was heaving, practically choking on the cold air by the time they stopped. It was darker than on the road with the trees blocking the majority of the moonlight.

"Why the fuck did you run?" Rob managed in between breaths.

Nathaniel slumped down with his back against a thick pine tree. Doug was pacing, his hands behind his round head as he walked.

"We need to go check on them," Rob said.

"No way," Nathaniel said, shaking his head. "I'm not going to jail. No college will accept me if there's an arrest on my records."

"What if the person is seriously injured and needs medical attention? Are you so selfish that you'd rather let them die?"

"I'm *not* going to jail," Nathaniel repeated.

"Will you both just shut the hell up for a second so I can think?" Doug shouted.

"You thinking is what got us here in the first place. I'm going to go make sure they're alright," Rob said.

Nathaniel shook his head and buried his face in his hands. Rob only took a few steps before Doug tackled him to the ground. Doug pressed his weight into Rob's stomach and restrained his hands above him.

"You're not going anywhere," Doug said.

"Get off of me."

A pinecone snapped behind them, sending a shiver down Rob's spine. Doug slid off him and stood up, but Rob didn't move. Every fiber in his body told him that he should be running, but he was paralyzed with fear. It was far too early for anyone else to be out in the woods and something in his gut told him it wasn't just an animal. A man limped into view with a sawed-off shotgun in his hands. Several glass shards were protruding from his skin, and his flannel coat was soaked in blood. Rob held his breath as the man lifted the shotgun towards Doug.

"Hey, take it easy man," Doug said. He held his arms in the air defensively and took a few steps backwards.

Without a word, the man pulled the trigger twice . Bullets tore through Doug's chest, spewing flesh and blood into the air. Nathaniel screamed as Doug's lifeless body fell to the ground. The man caressed the shotgun and limped towards Nathaniel. Nathaniel stood up on his shaky legs, but was blocked by a massive tree trunk as he attempted to take a step back.

"Please, sir, don't do this." Urine ran down Nathaniel's leg. "It was an accident, I swear."

A smile formed on the man's cracked lips. "An accident, huh?"

Nathaniel feebly nodded.

"Well, that would be a shame," he said, pausing next to Doug's body. "Considering your friend is already dead and all."

Nathaniel tried to run, but his foot caught one of the tree's massive roots and he fell onto the ground. The man shuffled over and pressed the barrel of the gun into his back. Nathaniel whimpered as tears slid down his cheeks. Rob remained still, unable to bring himself to his feet. It was like he was watching a bad horror film, only the man wasn't holding a prop gun and Doug wasn't pretending to be dead—he was *actually* dead.

"I don't want to die," Nathaniel whispered.

Shots rang out as the man pulled the trigger three times. Nathaniel cried and screamed until his own blood pooled and choked him. It was an awful sequence of sounds, but the silence that followed was worse. The man gripped the shotgun as he scanned his surroundings.

"I know you're there, boy. I can hear you breathing." He spat onto Nathaniel's body.

Rob slowly moved his hand over his mouth as the stranger reloaded his gun. His fingers were clamped down tight enough to lose circulation and his face ached. He wanted to believe the man wouldn't be able to find him, or that he wouldn't think he was guilty by association. While he wasn't the one who dumped the rocks, he didn't stop his friends either. A twig snapped in the distance and the man fired off another two rounds. He paused, as if he was waiting to see if he killed his target, and Rob decided to take his chance. He jumped up and took off running back towards the highway. The man flipped around and pulled the trigger, sending a bullet into Rob's left shoulder. He fell forward, throwing his hands in front of him to break the fall. His shoulder felt like it was on fire, overshadowing the pain from the burs and thorns stuck in his hands.

Before Rob could even attempt to stand, the man was already next to him with the gun aimed at the back of his head. He kicked Rob over so that they were facing one another.

"For a second I almost thought there were only two of you kids. Hell, if you hadn't had ran I might not have found you," the man said, laughing. "You kids have to pay for what you've done."

"Is that what this is? Some sort of fucked up vigilante justice?"

"You better watch your mouth boy."

"Fuck *you*."

Rob winced as the man pulled the trigger, but nothing happened. The man pulled it twice more, but again, nothing—he was out of shells. Rob grabbed the gun's barrel and thrust it back, nearly knocking the man down. He jumped up and started running again. Adrenaline pumped through his veins, making his strides long and fast despite his wound. The man chased after him as quickly as he could, but Rob was already at the edge of the woods. As soon as his boot touched the pavement of the service road, he was blinded by headlights. He had no time to react. His legs buckled as the Honda smashed into him and pulled him underneath it. He rolled several times before landing in the center of the lane. The vehicle's wheels screamed as it sped away into the night.

Rob's entire body was writhing in pain as he spat blood out onto the road. He slowly rolled himself over to find the man looming over him. His expression was no longer amused, instead it was serious and cold. He bashed the shotgun's handle into Rob's face over and over again until his vision blurred and darkness consumed him.

Guilty by Association was first published in The Sirens Call, Winter 2022 Issue 60 in December 2022.

12 ▌

Freak Accident

The interrogation room is cramped. A bulb in one of the light fixtures is flickering. The room, already cold, hums as the air conditioning switches on. There's barely enough room for the table and two chairs. On top of the table sits a manila folder, next to it is a small notepad, riddled with ineligible scribbles, and an audio recording device. Two men sit on either side of the plastic table. One, Herald Tripp, is a detective. He's older, probably in his mid-forties. His short brown hair is thinning. His mustache is peppered with grey hairs. The other, Noel Jenkins, is the accused. He's barely thirty. Dirty blond curls frame his boyish face. His appearance is too clean-cut, too mild to be sitting at that table. Handcuffs hang heavily on his thin wrists.

"You murdered a kid..."

Noel slams his fists onto the table, rattling the cuffs. "No, he murdered mine!"

The detective shakes his head solemnly. He opens the manila folder and slides a picture towards Noel. It's of a teenage boy, no older than seventeen. He has fiery red hair and a crooked smile. His round face is pimpled.

"Look at him."

His eyes, grey like the ocean, refuse to break contact with the detective's.

Herald grabs a fistful of Noel's hair. He shoves his face towards the picture. "I SAID LOOK AT HIM, DAMMIT."

Noel's breaths are quick and frequent. His eyes are tightly shut. There is an intense heat burning in the back of his head. The actions of the detective do not bring guilt or remorse, only despair. The soul sucking type of despair that one only feels after losing a loved one.

***

It was a warm October evening, the first day of opening weekend of the annual "Pumpkin Festival Fair". The county fairground was overcrowded with vendors, rides, and patrons. Fumes of freshly popped popcorn, fried pies and corndogs, cotton candy, and the less appealing sweat odor produced by the crowd, were carried through the fair by a faint breeze.

Fashioned in a red flannel shirt and faded blue jeans, Noel walked through the crowds. In one hand he held a half-eaten corndog, drizzled with mustard and ketchup, in the other, his son's small hand. It's a day shy of his son's eighth birthday. His eyes, grey like his father's, were wide and excited.

"Can we go on some of the rides next? Please?" he asked.

Noel smiled down at him. "Of course, Arthur."

Nearby there were ponies fitted in small saddles positioned under a tent, a kiddie pool filled with rubber ducks, a house of mirrors, a ring-toss tent, and a swing carousel.

Arthur pulled his father toward the swing carousel.

"This one?" he asked, wide-eyed and hopeful.

Noel bit his lip. The carousal was large, fitted with twelve swings. Patrons were shrieking and laughing as it rose and spun, the highest point reaching almost forty feet in the air. It screeched as the ride lowered and came to a halt. Those in line eagerly walked past the turnstile as the swings released their previous occupants.

"Maybe we should start with something else, how about a ride on one of those fine steeds? I think I saw bumper cars by the entrance too."

Arthur stomped his foot in the ground and crossed his tiny arms. "But I want to ride *this* one."

"I don't even think you are tall enough to ride this one buddy-"

"Actually, the height requirement is only four feet," a voice interrupted.

Noel turned to a teenage boy, who was manning the booth. The teenager wore a plain oversized purple shirt with a nametag that read, "Jerry". A matching purple cap covered most of his curly brown hair. His thin, pale arm pointed to the cardboard poster with a cartoon child and measurements painted on it.

"Why don't you come here, and we can see where you're at?" he asked.

Arthur ran to the sign, placing his heels against it. His head was barely two inches shy of the minimum. Noel took a deep breath and Arthur's excitement morphed into disappointment.

"Sorry son, looks like you're too short."

"But-but tomorrow is my birthday, and I-I..." tears welled up in his eyes.

"Nonsense. This thing is just for show, he can ride."

"What?" Noel and Arthur asked in unison.

Jerry smiled, his mouth full of braces. "Yeah. Come up here buddy."

Before Noel could protest, Arthur ducked under the turnstile and ran to a vacant swing. Jerry went over and helped strap him in. Noel walked to the metal fencing and grabbed Jerry by his arm.

"What do you think you're doing? I want him off this ride," Noel said.

"Hey, relax man, it's just a ride. He'll be fine."

Noel's grip tightened.

"Easy, that hurts," the teenager shuffled back. "Seriously dude, I've been working this ride every year since I was thirteen. I swear on my life, it's safe."

"Come on Dad! Please! I promise if you let me, I won't ask for anything else," a lone tear slipped down his puffy cheek. "You can even take back all my presents. Please? Pretty pretty please?"

Noel sighed and let go of teenager's arm. "Fine."

He relinquished two tickets to Jerry, but his disapproving expression remained. The teenager rubbed his arm before flipping the ride on. The ride screeched again as it rose and began spinning, slowly and then with speed. The top, painted red and gold and fitted with white lights, tilted left and right as it spun. A wide grin was spread across Arthur's face. He squealed like a pig as it picked up speed.

Suddenly there was a pop. It could have been mistaken for a firework or gun shot, but it had come from the carousel.

"What was that?" Noel asked.

Jerry looked at the ride. Before he could say anything, another pop. Arthur's squeals turned into screams. One of the chains connecting Arthur's swing had come loose. He was over on his side, as the other chain struggled to stay attached.

"Stop the ride! Do something!"

Jerry's eyes were wide with fear. The ride was at his highest point, almost to its top speed. His hand hesitated over the killswitch. Noel dropped the corndog as his hands clasped on the metal fencing, his knuckles were white.

"Stop it now!"

Jerry smashed the button as hard as he could. A third and final pop sounded. The second chain had broken free. Arthur, still belted into the swing, went flying. Everything was silent. Noel didn't hear the snapping of Arthur's neck as his head smashed against a metal pole, or the screams of the petrified onlookers. It was all silent.

***

"You've had a clean record until now," Herald releases his grip, "not even a single parking ticket. Maybe that's why you were caught. Clearly, you're not a criminal mastermind."

Noel pulls his head up. "I didn't care."

Herald takes a seat at the table. "Excuse me?"

"I didn't care if I was caught. Arthur is... was all I had."

The detective flips through papers in the folder, stopping at a file that has a woman's photo paper clipped to it. He carefully removes the photo and slides it in front of Noel. The woman is smiling in the photo. Her auburn-colored hair is pulled into a tight braid. Her face is slender, and her nose is similarly shaped to Arthur's.

"Do you think Elizabeth would've wanted this?" Herald asks.

"Beth would've wanted her son alive. You know what her dying wish was to me? To take care of him, show him all the things in the world she hadn't gotten the chance to," he fights the tears in his eyes. "When the doctor said her cancer was terminal, her first thought was Arthur. She spent her last few weeks writing him letters for me to give him as he grew up. One for when he went to college, his wedding day, his thirtieth birthday, the day he had his own kid, all the things he'll never get to experience."

Herald takes out another photo, one of Arthur. He moves the teenager's photo to the middle, placing the one of Elizabeth and Arthur on either side of it.

"You won't hear me say that I understand what you're going through. I'm married and my kids are all grown. I do empathize with you Mr. Jenkins. You're not supposed to bury your children," he pulls a cigarette and lights it, "but there's no justification for what you did."

***

It didn't take long for Noel to find out where Jerry lived. The story of "The Boy Tragically Killed at Family Carnival" was all over the internet and newspaper. Young Jerry hadn't commented on the ordeal, but his mother, Helena George, was quoted, saying "My son was and still is in shock. He did all he could."

One thing led to another. A quick Google search of "Helena George" brought up her real estate agency, her personal Facebook profile, and then the address where she lived with Jerry and his younger brother. The house was large and pristine, hidden in a gated community; however, the gated community didn't do a proper screening process when they hired their security guard, he was asleep at his post before it was even eleven thirty. Dressed in a black ball cap, black hoodie, black pants and sneakers, Noel slid by the sleeping man with ease. His fingers were tensely wrapped around the shoulder of his backpack strap.

The walk from the entrance to Jerry's house was almost peaceful. It was a cloudless night, and the moon was full, providing ample natural light. All the yards in the neighborhood were manicured to perfection, not a weed in sight. No dogs barked, not even the flicker of a lone television set, it was like they had their own curfew, and everyone was in a sleep as deep as the security guard's.

Jerry's house was at the end of a small cul-de-sac. Its exterior was composed of white stone and wood paneling. A wooden fence, tall and stained a tannish brown, surrounded the property. The gate latch was unlocked, like an open invitation for someone to break into the spacious backyard. The backyard itself was less tidy. A pool encapsulated the majority of the space. Innertubes and neon colored pool noodles swayed gently on the surface.

Noel sat down his backpack and began digging through its contents: a small knife, a tire iron, duct tape, rope, zip ties, and a newspaper. It was the same newspaper featuring the article about Arthur's death. He used the tire iron to break the glass of the back door. His hand cautiously unlocked the deadbolt, but no alarm sounded as he entered. Of course, they had an alarm system, but it had been left unarmed. Perhaps in some tired daze Ms. George thought she had turned it on, or maybe she thought the community was too safe to even bother.

It was dark, but he knew the floor plan, as *Zillow* had graciously provided interior pictures. The boys' rooms were upstairs, along with an open sitting area that doubled as a makeshift gaming room, and a small bathroom. He gripped the tire iron in his right hand and the stair railing with his left as he walked up the stairs. School pictures of the boys as well as a few of the entire family were nailed in the wall and ascended with the steps. A door creaked open, and Noel stopped. He was almost at the top of the stairs. Moonlight poured in through an open window, but it was still dark. Another door creaked. The sound of urine splashing echoed throughout the upstairs.

Noel took another step. He could clearly see the bathroom door. The handle itself was in arms reach. His heart felt like it was going to burst. A figure walked out of the bathroom, naked from the waist up. From his height and stature, it was obviously Jerry. With one swift move, Noel struck him in the back of the head with the tire iron. He went down without a scream or wail, only the thudding sound as his body hit the plush carpet.

The second thud came when Noel dropped the bloodied tire iron. It was louder. He bent over and grabbed Jerry by the ankles. He dragged him down the stairs, a trail of blood followed. The trail snaked around the backyard and into the front, stopping at a young oak tree. It was after one thirty in the morning by the time Noel had finally left.

He had taken his time positioning the body, he wanted to get it just *right*. Jerry's arms were outstretched, zip-tied to low branches. A rope fastened his torso to the trunk, another around his neck. The teenager's head drooped over. His eyes were open but glazed. The newspaper, turned to the article about the so-called accident, was tucked into the rim of his pajama pants. In large red sharpie, "MURDERER" was scribbled across his hairless chest.

***

"What happened to your son was a freak accident," Herald chews on the cigarette, "there was no reason for you to kill an innocent kid."

"Jerry was the reason Arthur died," Noel slams his hands down. "He knew Arthur was too short for that ride, but he told him he could ride it anyway. Had he just followed the guidelines, Arthur and Jerry would both be alive today."

Herald takes a deep breath and sighs. "Jerry is still alive today."

His words hit Noel like a punch in the stomach. Numbness takes over his entire body. There is no way he was alive when he left... *right*?

"What?"

"Noel, look at the photograph."

He forces his eyes down. Taken aback, he squints, as if he's not seeing the boy correctly. It's not a photograph of Jerry. Surely, his eyes must be playing a trick on him.

"Who is this?"

"Brandon McNeil."

"Why are you showing this kid to me?"

"The night you went to Jerry's, he wasn't alone," Herald flips to a blank page in the notepad, "Jerry's best friend Brandon was spending the night. You didn't kill Jerry, you killed Brandon."

Noel opens his mouth to speak, but nothing comes out. His throat is dry.

"Based on the medical examiner's report, what I believed happened was you came in, hit him from behind with a blunt object and left him to bleed out. You were so certain it was Jerry you didn't even bother to check the body. Like Jerry, Brandon had nothing to do with your son's death, he was just in the wrong place at the wrong time. Two innocent lives have been lost now."

Noel takes several quick, panicked breaths. He feels the heat rising to the back of his head once again. Arthur's lifeless body, still belted into the swing, flashes in his mind. He can hear the sirens from the ambulance, the stomping as the paramedics run over, and the zipper as it zips up the body bag.

"I'm done talking until my lawyer is present."

Freak Accident was first published in Broken by Design: A Short Story Collection in June 2021.

13 |

Ghosted

The first time Sarah saw Daniel was on Sunday, Mother's Day, and the department store was as busy as usual for a weekend. She was wearing a striped shirt and black skirt. Her long red hair was pulled into a tight ponytail. A walkie-talkie was fastened to the waistband of her skirt, a headset in her ear. She was working at the register, half-way through her six-hour shift when he stepped in front of her. The first thing she noticed about him was his smile. He had a beautiful smile. Whenever his lips curved, dimples would appear on both sides of his cheeks. The second thing she noticed were his icy-blue eyes. They were even more vibrant in person than his pictures on *Tinder*.

"I didn't see you walk in," she said.

Daniel smiled. "I know, you were with a customer."

He placed an oddly shaped toothbrush holder and a pillow on the counter. Sarah scanned the items as slow as she could. She wanted to talk to him for as long as possible, which probably wouldn't be long at all due to her manager, a middle-aged woman who was far from friendly, hovering by the line.

"It's good to actually *see* you," she said.

"I know. I could've waited until our date tomorrow, but I didn't want to. It's been two weeks already and that's long enough."

"Are you still okay with eating Mexican food?"

"Yes, so long as there's no guacamole."

"Why not? Please don't tell me you don't like guacamole, that *could* be a deal-breaker."

"Honestly, I'm allergic to avocados," he looked at her and smiled sheepishly, "but I would still kiss you if you ate guacamole. My face would probably swell, but it wouldn't matter, it would be worth it."

Sarah felt heat rush to her face. She didn't know what to say to that. Her manager seemed like she was eavesdropping, shooting a weird glance in their direction. The line was starting to wrap around. Sarah bagged his receipt with his items and handed him the bag. He lingered, as if he had more to say.

"I'm glad you came," she smiled. "You saved a whopping twelve dollars and forty-two cents today. There's a link for a survey at the bottom of the receipt in case you'd like to give us some feedback. I hope you'll come back soon."

He winked. "I'm sure I will."

About an hour after he left, Sarah's manager approached the counter. She had a piece of paper and for once, a smile on her face.

"Someone recognized you by name on the survey," she said.

Sarah's eyes widened. She had been working at the store for almost two months and had never been recognized before on the survey.

"What'd they say?"

The manager read the comment over the walkie-system for all the employees to hear, "Sarah is amazing. She is the reason I will come back."

A wide smile spread across Sarah's face and her cheeks flushed. She knew immediately that Daniel had wrote it.

***

They met at the town square for their first date. The square was a popular spot for college kids and elderly people alike. It was packed, especially for a weeknight. People flocked on the grass, cluttered the sidewalks, and filled the small shops. Jazz music echoed through the air. The sun was already setting, but it was still uncomfortably warm outside. Daniel was wearing a collared shirt, jeans, and sneakers. His golden hair, short and curly, was stiff with gel. Sarah was wearing a black dress with white polka dots. She had tried on about eight different outfits before deciding on that dress. She wanted to look perfect, or as perfect as she imagined she could. Her hair was curled. Mascara coated her eyelashes, and blush kissed her freckled cheeks.

"Sorry I'm late," she said.

He pulled her into a hug. His cologne was warm and inviting.

"Don't worry about it, I was early. I think we're going to have to go to a different spot though."

The Mexican restaurant had a sign taped to the window that said, "CLOSED for a private event."

"What were you in the mood for?" she asked.

He casually shrugged his shoulders. "Anything really. I don't know what's around here, so I'll go with whatever you pick."

Daniel had recently moved from Alabama. A recent college graduate, he had left everything behind to start a new job at a tech company. Besides a friend living a few cities away, Sarah was technically the only person he knew in Texas.

"Hmmm... How would you feel about a hamburger?"

"I'm always in the mood for a good burger."

They waded through the crowded sidewalk to get to LB's Burgers. It was a small and cozy burger joint. Lights were strung from the ceiling. Old country songs hummed in the background, mixing with the echoed conversations. They sat in a secluded booth on the second floor. The waitress brought a bowl of brisket queso and crisp tortilla chips. He talked fondly about elephants, and his time abroad in Thailand. She talked about her paintings, and her struggles to find a full-time job. She was nervous, but his smile and gentle laugh were enough to put her at ease.

After dinner they ventured to a craft bar. The bar was packed, but they were only focused on each other. Sarah bought the first round. A fruity cocktail for her, and a blonde beer for him. They went outside and sat on a wooden bench by the flameless fire-pit. Some eighties rock band blared from the speakers. Mosquitoes buzzed by, undeterred by citronella candles.

"What was your most embarrassing moment?" Sarah asked.

He furrowed his brow. "I have to think for a second."

Sarah stirred her drink. She was sweating as the sun's absence did little to curb the summer heat.

"I was in the car with my parents when my mom ran a stop sign. A cop pulled us over and while he was talking to my mom a girl from the front seat of the car said, 'Hi Daniel'. It was a girl I had ghosted my freshman year of college."

She laughed, a mixture of amusement and slight discomfort. Ghosting had always been one of her pet peeves and she was no stranger to it. She would rather have some form of finality, even if it was just a text message saying they weren't interested, anything was better than the silence.

"Did your mom end up getting a ticket?"

"Yes, she did."

They both laughed.

"I hope you don't ghost me," she said.

"Don't worry, I won't," he said.

She smiled and touched his thigh. Part of her felt stupid for even saying that. *Of course, he wouldn't.* How could someone who communicated with her on a daily basis just stop? He had a habit of texting her from the time he woke up until he went to bed. Even during work, he made time for her. It was still early in the relationship, but he seemed invested.

Daniel checked his watch. "It's almost ten o' clock. I hate to end things now, but I have to get up early for work tomorrow."

"I understand. Would you mind walking me to my truck? I will drive you to your car."

"Actually," he blushed, "I took an *Uber*. I wasn't sure how much I'd drink tonight and didn't want to drink and drive. I only live about ten minutes away, it's not a big deal I'll call another."

"That's not necessary. I'll drive you back."

"You sure?"

"Absolutely, I don't mind."

Getting to drive him meant they got to spend more time together, even if it was just a few minutes longer, she'd take all the extra time she could get. *Youngblood* played quietly in the background while he directed her.

They sat in her truck outside his apartment complex in silence. It was clear, neither of them wanted the night to end. Sarah's heart was pounding, and her palms were sweaty. She wanted to kiss him, but she was scared. Not scared that he was going to reject her but scared that she was going about it wrong. She didn't know how to bring it up and she didn't want to be impulsive either.

"I'd invite you in, but it's late and I know you have a bit of a drive home," he said.

Sarah nodded, she understood. Yet, neither of them moved. The truck was in park and they both still had their seatbelts on. He didn't reach for the door and she didn't bother to unlock it.

"This is kind-of-awkward, but," she swallowed the dry air in her throat, "I didn't eat any guacamole."

A sly smile formed on his lips as he unbuckled his seat belt. They leaned towards each other, over the console, and his lips pressed hard against hers. It wasn't like a normal first kiss. It had a kick to it. Warmth spread throughout her entire body. The more they kissed the more she wanted. She didn't want the date to end there but didn't stop him from getting out of the vehicle. She lingered, watching him slip through the parked cars until he went up the stairs and disappeared inside his apartment. She considered parking and going up after him but didn't.

Sarah lived about twenty minutes away from Daniel, and butterflies stirred in her stomach the entire drive home. He was special, different than other boys she had dated. He had potential, not just for casual dating, no, he had potential to be a serious boyfriend. Sarah hadn't been in a serious relation-ship for over a year. Sure, she had dated on and off, but no one was ever worth investing feelings into. It almost felt like she was destined to spend the rest of her twenties single.

Daniel texted Sarah before she had even got home. He said, "Hey I had a lot of fun with you tonight. You are so sweet, funny, and beautiful. Such a nice change from what I had come to accept as a date. I hope to see you again soon."

***

Their next date was scheduled to be at his apartment. Sarah had already been in town for a job interview, so she was just going to hang around until he got off work. The inter-view hadn't gone as she'd hope, but her spirits were still high. She may not have gotten the job, but she was going to see Daniel, so she didn't care. She went to a small grocery store and bought a bottle of white wine and a package of mixed cookies. He texted her when he left work and she drove over to his apartment to wait.

He had around a forty-minute drive back, so she just sat in her truck, air-conditioning blasting while she sang to *Bastille* songs until her throat felt dry.

"I'm here," he texted.

He arrived later than expected, but it was alright. She was just happy to see him. A smile was plastered on his face as he walked up to her truck. He wore a blue collared shirt and khaki pants. She was wearing a floral print t-shirt and lacy shorts. She got out and wrapped her arms around him.

His apartment was nice. The floor plan was spacious, a two-bedroom with two bathrooms, kitchen, dining area, and living room. There was a large cow painting on wooden boards hung up over the grey couch. An elephant picture, finger painted and bought from a street merchant in Thailand, was framed in the dining area.

"Do you mind if I take a quick shower? You can watch a show or something," he said.

"No, go for it."

She started the latest episode of *Westworld* and curled up on the couch. After his shower, he came out with a thick blue comforter-like blanket. He settled into the couch next to her.

"Do you want to start a movie?" she asked.

"No, we can finish this. I actually binged the series a few days ago so I could be up to date," he blushed. "I know how much you like it."

Is he serious? She rested her head on his shoulder. Heat was radiating off his body. She felt a little uneasy, unsure of what to say. She knew him but she didn't really know him. If she asked too many questions, perhaps he would find her annoying.

"Would you want to hang out again tomorrow or one day this weekend?" he asked.

"Three nights in one week? Won't you be sick of me?"

"I don't think that's possible."

When the show finished, they started watching a French horror movie on *Netflix* called *Raw*. Sarah's back was to his side and his arms were wrapped around her. She played with his fingers, part of her wanted to hold his hand, but she didn't. Again, fear. Fear that it was too soon, or that he would be uncomfortable. He caressed her arm and leg, only pausing to take sips of wine. His face contorted in disgust and horror as they watched the cannibals on the screen.

Suddenly, Daniel turned and started kissing her. It was just as electric as their first kiss. His hands caressed her sides. She slid her fingers underneath his shirt, pressing them into his back.

"Do you want to do this here, or in the bedroom?" he asked.

"The bedroom."

Hastily, he got up. She pulled off her t-shirt and followed him around the hall into his room. It was dark, so he turned on the light in his closet and cracked the door. The room was scarcely furnished with just a bed and a nightstand. Both the walls and carpet were white. A paddle from his fraternity days hung on the wall. She threw off her shorts and climbed onto the bed with him. She straddled him while they kissed, pausing only to remove her floral bra as he removed his shirt.

They shifted positions. She was on her back, and he was on top of and inside her. Her nails were pressed into his back. His fingers were tangled in her hair. Sweat beaded on their naked bodies. Their breaths were labored. Euphoria flowed throughout her entire body, thick like the blood in her veins. She didn't want him to stop.

Something seemed different. Daniel hadn't texted her when she got home that night. Sarah always felt uneasy after having sex with someone new for the first time. She had so many boys disappear after. They get what they want, and they're done. She didn't think Daniel was like that, but she was still worried. She hadn't known him for very long, but she was already getting attached. She didn't sleep at all that night. In the morning, her phone had no new messages or *Snapchat* notifications.

"Do you still want to hangout this weekend?" she texted.

"Actually, I have plans."

"No worries, maybe next week."

No response.

It wasn't like him to not respond, but she wasn't too worried. He was at work, and it was possible that he was too busy to text. She busied herself at home, working on a painting of a hummingbird. Her palette held only warm colors: yellow, red, and orange. In the late afternoon, she sent him a picture on *Snapchat* of her painting. He looked at the picture almost immediately but sent no response. *Relax. He's just busy, don't bother him.*

Saturday morning came without a "good morning text", and a knot was growing in her stomach. The guy who had texted her many good mornings and goodnights, suddenly wasn't there.

Work was slow, barely any customers, and it left her with little distractions. Her mind echoed with images of him. She felt his skin against hers and his cologne clogged her nose. She had let him in and carelessly got attached. The thought of him being like the rest, made her stomach twist. With no managers or customers nearby, she quietly pulled her phone from her pocket. No new text messages. Her *Snapchat* picture was still left on "opened".

"Hey can you be honest with me? I'd rather know so I can stop wondering and get on with stuff. Are we done? Feels like it's changed since Thursday night. I know you can get busy but even before you would still text me," she texted.

"Sorry I've been running around all day!"

"So I'm just being crazy?"

He didn't respond.

Ghosted was first published in Broken by Design: A Short Story Collection in June 2021.

14 |

The Wild

It's a muggy afternoon. The forest's trees are thick and full, but their shade does little to alleviate the heat, and Tom's body is ravaged in sweat. Humidity bogs his every movement. He doesn't know how long he's been walking, nor how long he's been on his own now. His legs throb relentlessly. An old, rusted axe is his only company, his fingers cramp around its splintered handle. There's a story behind this worn axe, how it came to be abandoned in a desolate forest, forgotten with time, until he, a strange man with no more than the torn clothes on his back, stumbled across it. Fondly, or perhaps because he had lost his mind, Tom had named the axe Mary, after his wife. His wife, he presumes by now, is under the impression that she is widowed. The war took her brother, and now the wild had taken her husband.

Tom finally surrenders to his legs' pleas by a large pond. Its water is murky with a stale odor, but the occasional rift hints at the presence of fish. Mosquito larvae dance underneath the surface. A small snapping turtle naps at the pond's edge. The ground is covered in crunchy fallen leaves; however, the turtle doesn't appear to have heard his steps. He crouches down and crawls towards the turtle. Still, it doesn't move. He draws Mary into the air before bringing her down into the turtle's shell. Its hisses don't dissuade him, again and again, he brings her down until the creature stops stirring. His hands lift the lifeless turtle into his lap, and with a loud crack, he breaks open its shell. Without hesitation, he digs his fingers into its back, pulling apart its rubbery meat. It's no five-star meal, but the bottomless pit that has replaced his stomach accepts it, nonetheless.

Tom wants to rest but he can't let himself. The sun lingers, but it won't be long before it retreats to the West, and he needs shelter. He has spent previous nights walking, occasionally climbing a tree to find sanctuary on one of its branches, but his strength has diminished with each passing day. There is no way he could climb a tree today. Besides, with the pond nearby, it's the perfect site to rest for a few days and recoup. Birds shriek overhead, the leaves protecting them from eyesight. The forest is densely populated with trees of all sizes, including saplings. With Mary by his side, Tom secures limbs, branches, and sticks. He collects stringy grass that once populated the pond's edges.

Mud is his glue, grass his nails, and branches his wood. He plants the thickest, strongest branches in the dirt as the frame for his shelter. One by one, he ties them together until there are three sides, each about six feet long. He slathers mud at the base and in between. He ties the medium-sized, leaner branches together like a raft and hoists them on top of the structure. Again, he adds mud. Similar to straw in a horse's stall, he beds the shelter with the pond's grass. On the fourth side he places shorter sticks. They are short enough for him to step over but high enough to keep out any unwanted critters. In all honesty, it isn't pretty, but it's sturdy and that's all that matters to Tom. Besides, he has never been a boy scout or anything like that. Tom grew up in the city. His only ties to the wilderness are camping trips when he was a teenager, but even those were tame. His family chose an RV instead of a tent, and they were always at a regulated and maintained state park, not out in the middle of nowhere.

Tom places rocks in an imperfect circle around a pile of sticks and dry leaves. The sun is now setting. The birds are quiet, no longer chirping, and he feels alone. It's not the "I'm the only person in this forest type of being alone", it's the "I'm going to die out here and no one will ever find me type of alone". He twirls a stick in his hands, pressing down. A whisper of smoke appears, and he rubs harder until it ignites. The fire grows and smoke travels towards the treetops. *Success*. He sits back and wipes the sweat off his brow. He feeds leaves and smaller sticks to the fire and it crackles with each gift. Besides the birds and his own thoughts, this is the only sound he's heard in days. It brings him a little bit of comfort.

Tom carries Mary into the shelter and lays her down beside him. His eyes are heavy, but he doesn't want to close them. Every time he shuts his eyes, he's brought back to the ship. No one in the crew had expected nor been prepared for the storm. It came without mercy and raged a war against them. The sails folded and crumbled, and the sea swallowed them whole. Tom had felt lucky, at first, waking up on the shore of this foreign island. He had waited for the others, surely they would wash up too, but only corpses and wreckage joined him. The smell of decaying flesh and salt water still burns his nostrils.

A twig snaps and Tom's eyes fly open. Instinctively, he grabs Mary. Over the past few days, he has seen varying tracks, some small and some ghastly, but he hadn't encountered anything. He had feared, sooner or later his luck was going to run out. He attempts to stand, but only makes it to his knees before the jagged tip of an arrow is pointed at his neck. The bow and arrow are wielded by a young exotic woman. Her dark brown skin is branded with scars. Her round face is framed by long black hair. She's adorned in animal pelts of varying shades and patterns. Underneath the pelts are a torn pair of khaki pants and a faded green button up shirt. Her brown boots are worn and muddied. A quiver is fashioned on her back.

"Drop it," her voice is low and cold.

Her eyes, like copper pools, glare at him. He lets Mary slip from his fingers. He's never been so scared, yet mesmerized, in his entire life.

"Out."

Holding his hands above his head, he exits the shelter. His eyes quickly scan his surroundings. There's no one else there, just the woman. A large bag composed from animal hide sits next to the shelter. A dead rabbit, already skinned, is propped up next to the dwindling fire. He sits down beside it. The woman adds stray twigs to the fire. It once again pops and crackles.

"M-my name is Tom. I was on an expedition to find new land when a storm hit, and we capsized. I'm the only survivor... I've been alone for days. I promise, I mean you no harm. What is your name?"

"I'm going to kill you, take this camp, and make it my own."

He feels a lump in his throat that isn't the turtle coming back up. *Kill?* He forces a nervous laugh, but she doesn't smile. She's serious. *She intends to kill me. Maybe I can change her mind? I have to try*. Being a middle-aged man with a receding hairline, Tom knows seduction isn't an option. He must use his wits if he's going to get out of this alive.

"If you were going to kill me, wouldn't I be tied up? I could escape at any moment..."

She raises an eyebrow. "Where are you going to go?"

Fair point, strike one. "If you kill me, you'll be all on your own again. You'll be... lonely. Yes, you'll be lonely."

"What makes you think I'm alone?"

He looks around. Nothing. No one else has shown up since he sat down and it is, besides the fire, eerily quiet. If she truly isn't alone, they would be here by now.

"I know, for a fact, that you're alone," he gestures to the rabbit, "not much meat for a group. Besides, if you weren't alone, wouldn't you already have a camp somewhere? Why would you need to take over mine... unless, you can't build one for yourself?"

She flinches. "I could build one if I tried."

"Then why haven't you? It looks like you've been traveling..."

"ENOUGH," she thrusts the arrow forward, pressing the tip against his neck again. Blood trickles down onto his collarbone. He closes his eyes and imagines his wife. He sees her plump face smiling, smells her lavender shampoo, and for a brief moment, he feels her soft hand over his. He waits for the sound of the fire to be replaced by her laughter. It isn't. He counts to ten. Still, no laughter, just crackling. Slowly, he opens his eyes, right first and then left. The woman has put the arrow back in its quiver and the bow down by her side. She is sitting on the other side of the fire, with her hands in her lap. She looks defeated.

"You're right, partially. I am alone, but I'm not lonely," she looks up and meets his gaze, "or at least I thought I wasn't. I haven't spoken to another human in so long, I forgot how much I missed it..."

Feeling relieved, Tom sighs. She lifts the rabbit and holds it over the fire. Her eyes are glazed over, as if she is seas away. He raises his hand to his neck. There's a cut, but it's small and insignificant. A mosquito buzzes by his ear.

"How long have you been out here?" he asks.

"I don't know."

"Days? Weeks? Months?"

She shrugs her shoulders. "I can't tell you. My story is similar to yours. I was working on a crew boat, we hit a storm, and somehow, I ended up here. There were others, but they didn't make it."

"What happened to them- Did you kill them?"

"No, I didn't kill them. I honestly can't tell you what happened to them, they just started disappearing one by one.

There was only ten of us to begin with, eight after the first night, and it just kept getting worse. People got paranoid, blamed each other, the group split up. It was just me and a little boy… he was with me for a few days, but then he was gone too. He left nothing behind except a trail of blood splatter."

"That's awful, I can't imagine," he shakes his head. "Why… why did you want to kill me?"

"Something about this island changes people. Maybe it's the realization that no one is coming to rescue you, but it has a way of making a person violent. I saw it firsthand before the group split up. I couldn't risk you turning on me, or worse, killing me."

"I won't, I can assure you that much. I think you're wrong, though. Someone will find and rescue us… you have to believe that."

She shakes her head. "I've been here long enough to know that's not true."

Tom opens his mouth to argue, but a twig snaps in the distance and silences him. Heat rushes to the back of his head and his stomach feels hollow.

"I thought you said you're alone?"

The woman shushes him. She drops the rabbit and cautiously picks up her bow. Tom's eyes dance wildly around. It's dark. The fire only provides ample light for about five feet before the trees merge with the darkness. Two amber eyes flash in the distance. A low growl echoes.

"Grab…your…axe…"

"What?"

"GRAB YOUR AXE!"

Tom rises, but before he can take, a step the amber eyes barrel towards him. It's a jaguar. The cat's ears are flattened against its head, claws out, and teeth bared. It's sleek, yet muscular. Clearly, the spotted cat hasn't missed any meals. A large scar is across its head, presumably the only damage left by its former prey. It knocks him backwards into the dirt. Tom throws his hands forward defensively and pushes with all the strength he can muster. It snaps at his neck and face, but he's able to hold it back. The jaguar's claws tear at his chest and arms. Each blow stings like a thousand hornets. Tom's blood is warm, but the piss that's pooling around his crotch is warmer. The woman launches an arrow into its flank. It whimpers and, as if Tom is already dead, turns on its haunches and abandons him for her. She manages to drive another arrow into the jaguar's shoulder before it's on top of her.

Tom's entire body feels numb, and he doesn't know if this is due to shock or if he's dying. The exhaustion that had plagued him earlier is tenfold. His vision is blurry, and the stars and treetops seem to melt into one. He wants to close his eyes and go to sleep, even if just for a second. He isn't afraid of seeing the ship or the corpses anymore. He's too tired for that. The woman screams, bringing all the feeling back to his body. Her words, "Grab your axe," are replaying like a broken record in his mind. *I'm not dead, yet.* He springs to his feet and runs towards the shelter. Clumsily he grabs Mary, her old handle is like a familiar friend. The woman attempts to use her bow to keep the jaguar at bay, but it's in vain, her skin tears with each swipe of its paw. Tom raises Mary with all his remaining strength and drives her down into the beast's spotted back. Blood spews as he pulls Mary from its back. The jaguar swipes its paw at Tom, catching his leg, but he doesn't stop. Again and again he brings Mary down. Each blow comes harder and faster. Blood stains her blade and his hands.

Suddenly, the jaguar falls limp and collapses onto the woman. Its snarls and hisses are no more, it's dead. Trembling, he drops Mary to the ground, and collapses to his knees. The adrenaline that fueled him is gone. His head aches and his breaths are labored. He pushes the jaguar off the woman and helps her sit up. Her breaths are labored too, but her injuries are more severe than his. Her blood pools on the ground, mixing with the jaguar's. She's fading, quickly, and the life is draining from her eyes. Tom pulls off his shirt, wads it up, and presses it against her chest. She weakly holds her hand up and points behind Tom.

"Run," she whispers.

"What?"

Tom turns to see several pairs of amber eyes glowing, all fixated on him. The woman says something else, but Tom doesn't hear her. He only hears the deafening sounds of the beasts as they barrel towards him.

The Wild was first published in Broken by Design: A Short Story Collection in June 2021

15

Toxic

It's a hot Saturday night. The sun has set, but the temperatures are still in the mid-eighties. Nevertheless, the Midnight Lounge bar is packed with customers. Most are college students as the bar is only about two miles from the local university. Mosquitoes are buzzing, but they're drowned out by the bar patrons' conversations, and *Immigrant Song* blaring from the speakers. Jess sits at a table by herself. She's wearing a denim baby doll dress, a sweater, and wedges. She's sweating, but she keeps her sweater on to hide the various bruises peppered on her arms. Her long auburn hair is pulled into a braid. She stirs her mojito with a straw. A pout sits on her thin lips, and she's visibly uncomfortable. *You can do this, you can do this, you CAN do this.*

"Hey, sorry I was running late!"

She turns to Richard and forces a smile. She had been hoping he wasn't going to show up at all. Richard is a short, slightly chubby, college-aged boy. Brown curly hair frames his freckled face. The humidity has his curls flat against his head. He's wearing a blue t-shirt with a shark wearing sunglasses on it, khaki shorts, and flip flops. Jess and Richard have been dating for several weeks and his outfit rarely deviates from a t-shirt and shorts.

"Don't worry about, I've only been here about fifteen minutes."

"Still! I'm going to grab a drink. Do you want one... or another one?"

She looks at her drink, which is almost full, and shakes her head. Richard goes to the counter. He is at ease as he talks to the bartender, talking to him as if he wasn't a stranger but a close friend. *He puts on such a good show.* He brings a white Russian back to the table. He pulls the cherry from his drink and pops it into his mouth.

"How've you been? Busy, I'm guessing?"

Jess nods. "Yeah, sorry I haven't been texting as much. I've just been working on this important essay for history that I procrastinated on."

"I was a little worried about you to be honest," he looks down at his drink. "After our last date went a little sour, I was surprised you invited me to come out tonight."

Sour? That's a funny way to describe you throwing me against the wall. "I'm sorry you were worried, I was just busy, I promise... What have you been up to?"

"Not much besides going to class and playing video games. Honestly, I've been slacking a little on my coursework. I know the semester is almost over, but I think there's still time to bring up my grades before finals... I've missed seeing you. I think Max misses you too. I swear he's been looking around my apartment for you, meowing at closed doors. If you haven't eaten, we could go back to my place? I have the ingredients for tacos."

"I would feel more comfortable if we stayed here."

Richard frowns, his disappointment apparent. The air around them is awkward and slightly tense. He takes a large drink, and Jess checks her phone. It's only been a few minutes, but it feels like they have been sitting there for hours. A bubbly group of coeds pass their table, their words are inaudible, but are a welcome distraction.

"Richard, we really need to talk."

"I think so too."

He reaches his hand across the table and places it over hers. It's rough and calloused, due to the years he spent enlisted in the Marines. He has always been open about his anxiety and PTSD brought on by his time in the service, but he uses it as an excuse. It's the reason he hits her. He never *means* to hit her, it's just a reflex, something she shouldn't take personally.

"I'm going to try and not beat around the bush. There's a reason I invited you out tonight. I want to talk about us..."

"Wait," Richard holds his hand up. "I think I know what you're going to say, and I've been feeling the same way."

"Really?"

"Yeah. It's crazy how we've only been dating for a few weeks, but it feels like I've known you for years. I've never met someone who *understands* me the way you do. I think, as you do too, it's time we take the next step. Jess, will you move in with me?"

Her mouth drops. She pulls her hand out from underneath his and grabs her mojito. She downs it, not pausing for breath. Her entire body is trembling. For a moment, she considers not pulling the trigger, but she knows she can't take another beating. Physically she's exhausted, mentally she's spent. *I'm safe, we're in a public place. I can do this.*

"Richard..."

His face is bright, beaming with hope. "Yes?"

"I didn't invite you out tonight to talk about furthering our relationship..."

"What?"

Suddenly, all eyes are on Jess. Not only is Richard focused on her, but the group of girls sitting nearby seem to be listening to the conversation as well. *Witnesses.*

"Richard, I want to break up."

His smile fades. "Why?"

You're an abusive asshole. "We're just... too different. I can't see us getting serious in the long run, I'm sorry."

He's silent for a moment, as if pondering her words. He mouths, "Okay," and nods his head several times. *Is this it? It was that easy?* He raises his glass, but instead of taking a drink, he throws its contents towards her. She has no time to react, and the melting ice and cool white Russian splatter her face and neck. It seeps into her dress and bra, and travels down her body. Everyone in the bar stares at them. One of the barbacks, a tall guy with a muscular build, rushes over. He offers a hand towel he'd been drying clean glasses with to Jess.

"Are you ok? What the fuck dude?" the barback glares at Richard.

Jess is speechless. She takes the towel and presses it against her damp face, a failed attempt to hide her tears. Her mascara smudges onto the towel. Richard sets his empty glass down harshly, meeting the table with a thud. He shrugs his shoulders nonchalantly, seemingly pleased with himself.

"Mind your own business, this is between me and my girlfriend."

"Ex-girlfriend," a blonde at a nearby table offers, "she just broke up with him and he freaked out."

"You stay out of this," Richard hisses.

"Alright buddy, you need to leave," the barback puts his hand on Richard's shoulder.

Richard throws his hand off of him. The man reaches again for his shoulder and Richard slaps it away. Several men, a mixture of bar patrons and employees, walk up behind the barback.

"This isn't up for debate, you're leaving *now*," the barback says.

Richard looks at the small group of men, most of them larger in size than he, and furrows his brow. He stands up and roughly pushes the chair towards the table.

"This isn't over," he says.

Richard walks to the fence and lets himself out. A few of the men follow, watching him walk until he's out of eyesight. The barback stays by the table. Jess is too embarrassed to look him in the eyes.

"Thank you," she says.

"You're welcome," he scratches the back of his head. "That guy seems like a real piece of work."

You have no idea. She hands the soiled towel back to him. She waits for him to walk off, but he doesn't. He takes the seat where Richard had been.

"My name is Michael. I don't mean to intrude, but are you okay? Do I need to call anyone for you or anything?"

She shakes her head. "I'm fine, but I think it's best if I just go home now. I do appreciate all of your help, though."

"At least, let me walk you to your car."

"I... walked. My apartment is just a few blocks away."

He rubs his temples. "Miss..."

"Jessica, but I go by Jess."

"Miss Jess," he smiles, "I cannot in good conscience let you walk to your apartment by yourself after that incident."

"What do you suggest I do instead? My roommate is out of town, and I can't think of anyone who would be able to drop everything just to come and take me back to my place."

"What if I were to drive you? I can get someone to cover the rest of my shift."

Get in the car with a stranger or walk home alone and risk running into Richard? She stares at him intently, taking in his appearance and mannerisms. *He seems like a nice guy, and there would be witnesses see him take me in case something happened.*

"I will let you drive me, on one condition," she says.

"Name it."

"You let me take a picture of your license plate AND your driver's license. Just in case you decide to kidnap me or something."

"Okay, but rest assured, I'm not in the kidnapping mood tonight," he jokes.

Jess climbs into the passenger seat of his white *Ford F-250*. She sets her purse down on the grey leather console. The truck is vacant save for a black backpack in one of the backseats and an empty *Chick-Fil-A* cup in the cup holder. A cartoon-style Edgar Allan Poe air freshener hangs from the rearview mirror. *Pompeii* plays quietly on the radio.

"I know you said it's just a few blocks away, but I think it would be better if I drove you," he says.

She nods and Michael drives the truck out of the bar's parking lot. Both sides of the street are packed with parked cars. The sidewalk is busy with drunk and sober individuals alike. Jess looks for Richard among the crowds, afraid he's out there waiting for her, but doesn't see him. She pulls off her sweater and folds it into her lap. Michael briefly glances from the road to her arms, but she doesn't notice. Her skin is pale, and the bruises are a stark contrast.

"Are you hot? I can turn the air conditioning up if you'd like."

"I'm fine, I just needed to take it off."

Silently, Michael drives to her apartment complex. The radio is on, but it's low and barely audible. He parks his truck against the curb, despite the "no parking" sign. Jess grabs her purse and unbuckles her seat belt, but he doesn't unlock the doors.

"Did... did he give you those?" he asks.

Jess looks down at the floorboard, ashamed. "Yes."

"Jesus. Have you told anyone about this?"

"My roommate knows, but that's about it. My parents live about four hours away, if I told them they'd make a big deal out of it and drive down. It's not that big of a deal, I just want to forget about him and move on with my life."

"No, it *is* a big deal. Abuse isn't a joke. I'm afraid he's not going to let you forget about him so easily."

"Why do you care? And what makes you say that?"

Michael points to the sidewalk. Richard is standing at the corner of the street, waiting in front of her apartment complex. He's glaring down at a cellphone in his hand. Jess takes her phone out. There are nine missed calls, and forty-seven unread text messages all from Richard. She doesn't have to read them to know what they say. The early messages will say he's sorry, and then they'll turn to rage and blame. She slides her phone back into her purse and sighs.

"For the record, I care because I have a little sister and if she was ever being abused, I'd want someone to look out for her," Michael strums his fingers on the steering wheel. "Have you eaten?"

"No."

"Okay, let's go get something to eat. If he's still here when we get back, I'll take care of it, okay?"

Jess nods. She buckles her seat belt and pushes her purse back onto the console. Michael turns his truck and merges back onto the road. Richard doesn't seem to notice her as they pull away. His focus completely on his phone. Still, his presence makes her uneasy.

"If you're right... and he doesn't go away, what then?"

Michael smiles. "Trust me, after I'm through with him, he won't *ever* bother you again."

Toxic was first published in Broken by Design: A Short Story Collection in June 2021.

16

Curiousity

It was a cold December morning, especially for Texas. Frost was dusted atop the grass and stuck to the windows of all the vehicles in the apartment complex's parking lot. Ava stood in front of her window, listening for any sign that her roommate was home, but the only noise was from the heater. Laura hadn't come back after her six o'clock final last night, and Ava's boyfriend Brad hadn't been responding to her texts. She didn't know if the two events were related, but it didn't sit well in her stomach. Suddenly her phone buzzed from on top of her dresser. She scrambled, nearly tripping over her orange tabby cat Merlin, and yanked it into her hand. Her smile faded. It was text from her mother, asking when she'll start her six-hour drive home.

"Soon," she replied.

Ava sighed and picked up Merlin. He purred softly as she put him into a plastic grey crate. She slipped her duffel bag over her shoulder and took one last look at her room. A picture of her and Brad caught her eye. They're standing outside a crowded bar with his arms wrapped around her, and they're both smiling. It was from a happier time, when they had only been dating only for a few months. She made the short walk down the stairs and to her red *Ford F-150*. She can't help herself from searching the lot for Laura's car, but it wasn't there. Merlin meowed from his carrier as the truck heated up. Ava's pale fingers strummed the steering wheel.

"We'll be home in a few hours Merlin, but I have one stop to make first. I can't go all break wondering," she said.

Christmas music softly played on the speaker as she turned out from the parking lot. The roads were quiet, atypical of the college town, but with the last of finals finished a day earlier most of the students were probably already on their way home for winter break. Already finished with her finals, Ava had considered leaving two days ago herself; however, with a slight suspicion and icy road conditions, she had delayed her trip until today. Brad's fraternity house was only a ten-minute walk or a five-minute drive, but each passing minute felt like an eternity. The closer she got the more her stomach twisted itself in knots.

Ava hesitated at the stop sign before his house, briefly considering turning around and getting on the highway to head home. *Maybe not knowing would be better*. A car pulled up behind her and laid on the horn. Slightly frazzled, she slammed her foot on the gas and her truck lurched forward.

"Guess, I have no choice now," she said.

Laura's old *Mustang* was parked outside of the fraternity house, and Ava's heart fell to her stomach. Brad wasn't the perfect boyfriend, he never had been, but Ava cared about him, nonetheless. The arguments seemed to be more frequent these past few months, and with his wandering side-eye, she knew the relationship was on the verge of ending; however, it didn't make her feel any better about him cheating on her with her roommate of all people.

The front door was open, and Brad and Laura were standing on the porch. He had one arm wrapped around her thin waist and the other pressed against the side of her face. Slowly, he leaned in and kissed her. Tears stung Ava's eyes. She rolled down her window and pressed her hand as hard as she could on the horn, making both Brad and Laura jump. They both looked at Ava's truck and their smiles disappeared. Their expressions flashed from guilt to shock, and from shock to concern. Brad dropped his hands and started briskly walking towards the road.

"Fuck you," she yelled with her middle finger up in the air.

Brad ran after her shouting her name, his shoes slipping on the slick ground, but she didn't stop. Instead, she rolled her window back up and turned the volume up on the radio. She was crying, not only because she was sad, but because she was angry as well. Angry for all the time she wasted with Brad, and angry for how she had considered Laura to be one of her closest friends. Her phone started ringing, barely audible over *Run Rudolph Run*. She reached into the passenger seat and grabbed it to see it was Brad calling. Not one ounce of her wanted to answer it. There was nothing he could say to make her understand or to forgive him- it was over. She turned her phone to silent, rolling past a stop sign when she did, and an eighteen-wheeler crashed into the side of her truck. Ava's ears rang as the truck rolled several times before settling into a ditch. Glass was everywhere, and blood oozed from Ava's nose and forehead. Merlin cried helplessly from his crate as Ava closed her heavy eyes.

Curiosity was first published in Broken by Design: A Short Story Collection in June 2021.

17

Killer Date

Ryann sat in front of her laptop in the darkness of her bedroom. The only light was provided by her computer screen and the television on her dresser which was tuned into a show about unsolved mysteries. She bit her lip, trying to conceal her frustration as she scoured through *Google* for information she could use in her thesis paper. This was Ryann's fourth year in graduate school. Her psychology program could've easily been completed in two years; however, she had been putting off writing her thesis paper. It was by the prompting of her program advisor, and her desire to stop funding her procrastination, that she finally decided it was time. This was, fingers crossed, going to be the last semester The University of Arizona got anymore tuition from her.

Kennedy, Ryann's longtime friend and roommate, stopped outside of her door. Her long blonde hair was curled, and she wore a mini dress and heels. She flipped the light switch on and the harsh contrast forced Ryann to blink rapidly until her eyes had fully adjusted. "Seriously?"

"What are you doing in here in the dark?" Kennedy asked.

Ryann didn't bother looking away from her screen. "Researching serial killers."

"Charming," she crossed her arms. "Did you forget about our plans tonight?"

".... no."

"Ry!"

"I'm sorry, I've been trying to get started on this damn thesis... What were we supposed to do tonight?"

"Of all the times, *now* you decide to actually start writing your thesis? You're hopeless," she sighed. "We're supposed to go on the double date with Collin and Hayden tonight- remember?"

Collin was Kennedy's serious boyfriend. They had been dating for over four years, and it felt like it was only a matter of time before he popped the question. Hayden was Collin's "sweet" and "attractive" friend who'd "be perfect for you," according to Kennedy. Ryann wasn't sure if this set up was to curb Kennedy's guilt about moving out in a few weeks to live with Collin, or if it was another one of her attempts to get her a boyfriend so she'd have a reason to get out of the house aside from school and work.

"Oh right, the date, I didn't forget. What time are we meeting them again?"

"We're supposed to be there in thirty minutes."

"I can do that. I'll start getting ready now, it'll only take me a few minutes."

Kennedy eyed Ryann's casual clothes, athletic shorts and an old band t-shirt, with her lips pursed. Ryann suddenly felt self-conscious.

"I can be ready soon, I promise."

They arrived at the bar only five minutes late, which had surprised them both. Ryann had changed into a lace crop top and jean shorts. The sunflower tattoo on her thigh was partially visible underneath the cuff of her shorts and was vibrant against her pale skin. Her short brown hair, styled in a bob, was straightened. She had, due to Kennedy's insistence, worn makeup; however, she was less interested in going on this date than she was about writing her thesis, and that spoke volumes.

Collin and Hayden were sitting outside in the bar's patio area at a wooden picnic table. It was packed with college kids drinking cheap beers, playing *Cornhole*, and swatting away the occasional thirsty mosquito. The September air was muggy and humid, and Ryann was already sweating by the time they walked over to the table.

"Hey babe," Collin said.

Collin was a former college football player turned bodybuilder. He was of average height but was insanely muscular. He had short red hair and his skin was unnaturally tan. His typical outfit consisted of a muscle-tee, athletic shorts, and never without his dirty white *Nike's*. He looked monstrous standing next to petite Kennedy. On the other hand, Hayden appeared to be his opposite. He was tall and lean with curly black hair almost as long as Ryann's. Both of his arms were covered in tattoos and his slender face was brushed with stubble. He wore jeans, boots, and a solid black shirt. His earthy cologne was strong, but not overwhelming.

"Hayden this is my girlfriend Kennedy and her roommate Ryann," Collin said.

"Hi," Hayden extended his hand to Ryann. "It's nice to meet you."

Ryann shook his hand. "Nice to meet you too."

"How about we go grab some drinks and food for the table while they get acquainted?" Kennedy winked at Collin.

"Of course."

Kennedy looped her arm with his and they headed towards the door to the inside of the bar. Ryann sat down on the opposite side of Hayden.

"They're not good at being subtle, are they?" Hayden asked.

Ryann shook her head and laughed. Hayden laughed too, revealing his dimples as he smiled. *Kennedy wasn't kidding about him being attractive.* She felt her cheeks redden and hoped her blush was enough to mask it.

"So, Collin tells me you're a graduate student at The University of Arizona? What are you studying?" Hayden asked.

Ryann nodded. "Psychology. I'm actually trying to complete my thesis so I can hopefully graduate in December."

"What's the topic of your thesis?"

"I plan on researching serial killers to see if there is a common behavior between them, and if their actions could've been predicted and possibly prevented. I've settled on a few names like the BTK Killer, and Ted Bundy, but I've just started looking... like literally today."

"That sounds intriguing. It would be nice to know if people are born monsters..." he trailed off, his eyes fixated on something in the distance.

Ryann fought the urge to turn to see what he was intensely staring at. She felt slightly uncomfortable and wished Kennedy and Collin would hurry up.

"I'm sorry I spaced out there for a moment, what were we speaking about?"

"Serial killers."

"Oh right," he smiled. "I would suggest looking into Ed Gein, he's my favorite serial killer."

"Didn't he inspire the *Texas Chainsaw Massacre* movies?"

"Yes, but I don't think they did his story justice. Are you going to try and find a local serial killer you can talk to? Maybe get inside their head?"

"I mean, I'd really rather not run into one in person."

Hayden laughed. "Well I'm sure you *could* find one out of jail, but it would be safer finding someone online and sending them a letter."

"Oh," her cheeks reddened again. "Like a prison pen pal?"

"Exactly. I wouldn't be surprised if you were able to find someone here in Arizona, too."

Kennedy and Collin returned to the table with a pitcher of some blue alcoholic concoction, four glasses, fried pickles, and chips with salsa. Kennedy sat down next Ryann, and Hayden scooted over so Collin could sit next to him. There was a smudge on Collin's neck the same shade as Kennedy's lipstick.

"What have you two been talking about?" Kennedy asked.

"Serial killers," Ryann said with a smirk.

Kennedy gave her a we-will-talk-about-this-later look but forced a small chuckle. More comfortable with her friend by her side, Ryann grabbed one of the fried pickles and slipped it in her mouth.

It was late by the time Ryann and Kennedy got back home. Their house was the only one on the street with its lights still on. Although a little buzzed, Ryann wasn't tired. She immediately grabbed her laptop off the floor and hopped on her bed. She typed, "Prison pen pal" into *Google* and several pages pulled up. The first website she clicked had the ability to filter through prisoners by their age, gender, location, ethnicity, and religion. Information about the prisoners, ranging from personal interests to public information about their crime and sentences, was available to view.

Kennedy stopped in front of Ryann's doorway. Her makeup was smudged and her hair slightly tangled- no doubt the result of quickie in the car with Collin.

"I suddenly understand why you're single," Kennedy said.

"What drove you to this conclusion?"

"You spent your first date talking about murderers and boring papers."

Ryann shrugged. "He asked for my phone number, so it wasn't *that* terrible."

Kennedy clumsily walked over, nearly slipping out of one of her heels. She balanced herself against the bed's headboard, so she was at eye-level with Ryann. Her breath reeked of tequila.

"What are you doing?"

"Research," Ryann closed the computer. "Go to bed, you're drunk."

Kennedy mumbled something ineligible before patting Ryann on the shoulder and leaving the room. Her heels knocked on the wood floor with each sluggish step she took, stopping only when she reached her own room down the hall. Ryann sighed and opened her laptop back up. She set Arizona as the location but left the other search fields blank. Thousands of results came up, men and women of all ages with different crimes. *This is going to take too long.* She opened another tab, and typed in, "Serial killers in Arizona."

The first link was to a story about Edgar Greene, a name Ryann remembered from the news headlines years earlier. He was a man from Mesa, Arizona, who had been convicted of murdering his parents, grandmother, and two younger siblings during Thanksgiving dinner. All five of his family members had died from gunshot wounds, their bodies slumped around the dinner table with no apparent attempt to escape their murderer. Blood and brain matter were splattered about the room. The police had found Edgar sitting outside on the porch covered in blood and cradling a sawed-off shotgun.

At the age of thirty-three, he was convicted of five counts of first-degree murder and sentenced to death. It had been more than two years since the guilty verdict and Edgar was still sitting on death row; however, his lawyers were feverishly attempting to appeal his conviction.

"Edgar was a decorated soldier who had spent two tours in Iraq and suffers from depression and severe PTSD. He should not have been convicted by reason of insanity," one of his lawyers was quoted.

Ryann scrolled down the page, scanning through the article and supposed evidence that was ignored by prosecutors. Edgar didn't look like a serial killer, not from his pictures where he stood next to those he murdered, nor in his mugshot. He was thin with high cheekbones and his blue eyes were big and doe-like without any hint of malice. Then again, neither Dahmer nor Bundy looked like murderers either.

Ryann switched back over to the pen pal site and narrowed the search filters to males in Arizona between the ages of thirty and thirty-six. Edgar was at the bottom of the third page, his picture was him standing in front of a white wall in his prison jumpsuit. His thin lips curved into a thin, smirk like, smile. It made her feel uneasy, as if he were staring at her face-to-face rather than an image on her computer. Ryann's phone buzzed and she nearly sprung out of the bed. She laughed, partially at herself and partially for her uneasiness, before fishing her phone out of her purse. There was text message from an unknown number that said, "It's Hayden. I had a great time tonight, and I will see you again soon."

A crash echoed throughout the home followed by the sound of glass shattering. Ryann calmly sat her phone down.

"Kennedy are you alright?"

No response other than muffled footsteps and glass crunching.

"You're supposed to be in bed," Ryann rubbed her temples. "I swear to God if you broke another lamp, I'm not paying for it."

Suddenly, there was a high pitch scream and Ryann jumped. If Kennedy thought she was being funny, she wasn't. Ryann slid off her bed and walked over to the hallway. It was pitch black save for a small blue nightlight. No light peeked from underneath Kennedy's bedroom door nor the bathroom. *Where are you?*

Another crash sounded along with a loud thud, as if something was slammed against a wall. Ryann felt her heart beating quickly in her chest. The hairs on the back of her neck were raised. Part of her felt silly, as Kennedy was drunk, and Ryann's imagination was probably playing a cruel trick on her.

"What are you do- Stop! Let go of me," Kennedy screamed.

Two gun shots tore through the night and Kennedy stopped screaming. Ryann's blood ran cold. It was eerily quiet, as the air conditioning wasn't running and not even the crickets were chirping. There was a loud screech, signaling Kennedy's door being opened. She flipped around, grabbed her phone, and ran to the window. Footsteps in the hall drew closer as she struggled to open the window. *Come on, please.* Finally, the latch gave and she slid it open. Ryann pushed through the screen and jumped out, hitting an overgrown bush before landing on the damp ground. She ran towards the front of the home. A shiny black *Mustang*, Collin's car, was parked in front of their house. *Thank God, he's still here.* Ryann let out a small sigh of relief and rushed to the car.

"Collin," she banged on the driver's side window. "What are you doing? I think Kennedy's been shot. We need to get help."

No answer. His appearance was masked by the heavy tint of the window. Ryann grabbed the door handle and was slightly surprised to find it unlocked. She opened the door and screamed. Buckled into his seat as if he was about to make the twenty-minute drive home, Collin sat with his head split wide open. Damp blood covered the leather seats and steering wheel. She didn't have to check for a pulse, she already knew he was dead. Ryann fell to her knees and vomited onto the pavement. *This can't be real. I must be dreaming.* She pinched her arm as hard as she could, leaving indentions in her skin, but it was in vain. She wasn't waking up and this wasn't a dream.

Ryann willed herself to stand and looked cautiously looked around. There was no way the killer hadn't heard her scream, but she didn't see anyone. Not even the neighbors had appeared to be disturbed as their lights were still out. Only the faint glow from the thin moon and the yellowed streetlight illuminated the neighborhood. Ryann shakily held her phone up and dialed 9-1-1.

"9-1-1, what is your emergency?" an operator asked.

Before she could answer, a gloved hand slipped over her mouth and knocked her phone onto the ground. Hot breath pressed against the back of her ear as the grip around her tightened. The smell of a familiar earthy cologne enveloped her, and her eyes widened.

"I told you I would see you again soon," Hayden whispered.

Killer Date was first published in Broken by Design: A Short Story Collection in June 2021.

18

Nine Lives

It was a chilly October night. The sky was cloudless, and the stars were vibrantly illuminated, outshining the thin crescent moon. The beauty of the stars was a stark contrast to the playground which, once a brightly painted and a popular spot for children, had dulled and been forgotten with time. Rosie sat in one of the swings on the playground's old swing set. Her long brown hair was pulled into a loose braid. She wore jeans and a solid black hoodie, something hard to spot without a light. Her tan fingers were interlaced with the rusted chains, and tears stained her cheeks. She pulled out her phone to check the time- almost nine o'clock in the evening. There were eighteen unread text messages, twenty-seven missed calls, and eight voicemail messages, all from her roommate Sarah. She didn't need to read the texts or listen to the messages to know what they say. She'd been gone for almost two hours and Sarah had to have found the note by now.

This night had been planned for weeks. With train tracks only a stone throw from her apartment complex it was easy to document the train's comings and goings. She had stayed up numerous nights, sitting on the balcony with a notepad in hand as she waited for the sounds of the trains. Every night without fail, a train rolled through around nine-fifteen, eleven-thirty and then again at two in the morning. Aside from the schedule she had to figure out where she was going to do it. She didn't want to be too close to her apartment where Sarah or another friend might find her, she didn't want to put them through that, but she had to find a spot where *someone* would find her. The railroad crossing behind the old elementary school, just before the creepy gas station that somehow managed to stay in business, was the spot she had settled on.

Her phone started chiming, the fifteen-minute warning for the nine-fifteen train's arrival. She had set an alarm for fifteen, ten, and five minutes beforehand, as if she would somehow forget. Could someone really forget to commit suicide? It's not a decision made on a whim, no, it was something Rosie spent countless hours thinking about over the course of many months. The emptiness inside her had grown far too powerful for her to dismiss, and her will to live had evaporated with each passing minute she spent without Landon. He was the love of her life and had been her everything. The day he died, her future died with him.

Rosie pushed her phone back into her pocket and stood up. She waded through the uncut grass in between the playground and school building. It was dilapidated, carelessly abandoned more than twenty years ago after a bigger school was built to accommodate the town's growing population. The windows were gone, and the elements had wreaked havoc on the inside, leaving it hazardous; however, the city was too lazy to tear it down and left it for the wildlife and occasional homeless person to inhabit. Something squeaked from within the tall grass and stopped Rosie in her tracks. She waited a few seconds before taking another step, and it squeaked again. Curious, Rosie pulled her phone out and turned on its flashlight. A small pair of glowing eyes were staring at her.

Before she could take another step, her phone started chiming- the ten-minute reminder. She quickly muted it, but the squeaking animal was already running towards the playground. It stopped underneath the contorted jungle-gym and Rosie could clearly see it was a small kitten. The kitten was a grey tabby with green eyes. It was emaciated with its large head appearing almost cartoonish attached to its thin body. Some sort of goop was caked around the kitten's eyes preventing them from opening more than halfway. Rosie turned back towards the road, but the kitten squeaked again, and she stopped. She only had nine minutes before the train arrived, but something about the pitiful creature made her hesitate.

Rosie walked over to the playground and kneeled in the old sawdust shavings. "Come here kitty."

Rosie extended her hand and the kitten cautiously approached her. It purred softly as it rubbed its thin body against her knees.

"What am I supposed to do with you?"

She knew it would die if she left it behind, but if she tried to get it help she would lose her only chance. Sarah had probably already notified the campus police. No one would look at her the same, and it would be worse than what it was already. Then again, could it actually get any worse? Rosie had always felt like she was alone, even in a room full of people. It was almost as if she had to put on a charade to make her friends think she was okay: she told as many jokes as she could, smiled the biggest, and made sure to keep her struggles to herself. Landon was the only person she didn't have to pretend around. He made her feel noticed, as if she did matter. Why was the universe so cruel to take away the one person in her life she truly needed?

Her phone started chiming- the five-minute warning. It wouldn't be much longer until the train rolled through town. She stood up and looked towards the road that led to the railroad crossing. Tonight was supposed to be the last time Rosie would hear the train's horn. She would put in her headphones, turn up the volume as high as she could, and walk the tracks as she listened to her favorite songs one last time. Rosie walked to the road, and the kitten followed closely behind. She looked down and it squeaked at her, making her smile. In regard to what came after death, Rosie wasn't sure what she believed, if anything; however, if she was conscious of life after death- she wouldn't want to know the kitten was starving, waiting endlessly until death finally claimed it too. She didn't believe it deserved to die, and she didn't want it to.

"You've been alone for a long time, haven't you?" She picked the kitten up and cradled it in her arms. "I know what that's like, and it's not something I would wish on anyone- or anything."

Rosie pulled out her phone again and dialed Sarah's number. Tears glistened in her eyes. The uncertainty of what would come next, frightened her more so than the uncertainty of what death would be like; however, she realized, just like the little kitten, she needed help. She had struggled far too long on her own. The train horn blew as she started walking back towards her apartment complex.

Nine Lives was first published in Broken by Design: A Short Story Collection in June 2021.

19

His One Mistake

The entire house is dark. A woman is asleep in a queen-sized bed in a small room. It is her childhood bedroom, where she has lived since the age of six. She is in her mid-twenties now, a recent college graduate caught in the limbo of early adulthood, where a degree is cherished but not enough to secure a well-paying job. Her thin arms are wrapped around a stuffed bear. Her blonde hair is a tangled mess around her thin face. It's nearly three o'clock in the morning. A young male lifts the rug embroidered, "Wipe your paws," and takes the spare key. The door squeaks as it opens and a large hound rushes at him with its lip curled back, and teeth bared. With all his strength, the man hits the dog with the butt of his pistol. The dog whimpers and falls to the floor unconscious.

The man casually strolls through the house. His fingers, covered by woolen gloves, touch the walls, frames, and shelves, as he walks through the home. He has been inside this house a countless number of times over the years, but never this late at night, and never without permission. He knows where to find the master bedroom, guest bathroom, and the two smaller bedrooms. His target is the bedroom where the woman sleeps. He knows its pink walls, hanging posters, shelves and picture frames. He happens to be in one of those picture frames, standing next to her with a wide grin on his face. A plush and carpeted rug lines the hallway, muting his shuffled steps. He enters her bedroom, and the smell of an unlit vanilla candle welcomes him.

The man withdraws a jagged knife from his pocket. Its touch brings him ecstasy, and his heartbeat races. He isn't naturally violent, he just likes to be in control. People are easy to control once they're afraid. He knows knives induce fear, it's part of their nature. The woman must be a heavy sleeper, as she doesn't stir when he wraps his left arm around her, nor when he slides his right hand under her neck, pressing the knife's blade softly against her skin. His hot breaths tickle her ear, but she stays asleep. It isn't until he whispers, "Wake up, sleeping beauty," that she groggily opens her eyes.

She attempts to turn her body, probably to see who is holding onto her, but his grip prevents her from moving. The woman's parents are out of town, visiting her younger brother who is still in college. The man has waited for weeks for an opportunity like this. Perhaps he wouldn't have even known about their planned absence had it not been for *Facebook*. Warmth radiates off his body and she is sweating under the pale pink comforter. She tries to move again but his hold only tightens.

"Chris stop, this isn't funny."

A wild grin spreads across the man's face. "Guess again."

Her eyes shoot open, and she lurches forward, knocking the stuffed bear onto the ground, and pushing the knife into her throat. She whimpers as the blood slips down onto her sheets. She tries to turn and look at her assailant, but it's in vain. His grip is too tight, and it's too dark to see anything anyway.

"I wouldn't do that if I were you," he says.

"Please don't hurt me, I don't have much, but you can have anything. Just promise me you won't hurt me or my dog."

"Too late for that," he chuckles, "but if you do everything I tell you, it won't be painful. Understood?"

Tears slide down her cheeks. "Y-yes."

"Get up, slowly."

He pulls back the knife and releases his grip. She unbundles herself from the covers and sits on the side of the bed. Her phone glows and buzzes on the nightstand. A text message from an unknown sender.

"That's... my boyfriend. He's supposed to come over tonight. You should leave before he gets here..."

The man rolls his eyes. "Chris isn't coming. He had some *problems* of his own."

Suddenly, she grabs the phone. It's in her hands before he could stop her. He reaches for her arm, but she lunges forward and breaks his grip. She runs out the bedroom. *Dammit.* He chases after her. She goes straight for the backdoor, but trips over her dog's lifeless body, and slams into the wall. Her phone slides out of her reach. He kicks it away and grabs her by her long hair. Her crying intensifies as he drags her back down the hallway and into the bedroom. Her fingers dig into the rug, dragging it with them.

He throws her into the bedroom and shuts the door. Her body hits the floor with a loud thud. She pulls her knees into her chest. He couldn't see her face, but he knows what she is thinking. *She wants her precious boyfriend to break down the doors and come and save her. If only she knew.*

"I said this didn't have to be painful Lisa."

"Why are you doing this? Who are you?"

"I'm surprised you don't recognize my voice. We've been *friends* for what, years? Perhaps it's because Chris. You seemed to forget everyone you supposedly cared about after I introduced you two."

"What.... Jason? No...."

Jason walks to her nightstand and flips on her lamp. She gasps even before he turns around. His tall, thin figure is recognizable. It didn't matter that a hat covers his greasy brown hair, there's no way she couldn't have known it was him. Her facial expression is torn between sadness and betrayal. It's genuine shock, as he knew it would be. After all, who would suspect their friend of fifteen years to break into their home, and threaten them with a knife? Jason had been her first friend when she moved to his small town. Their friendship had survived elementary, middle, and high school. It wasn't until Jason introduced Lisa to his friend and roommate Chris that their friendship had begun a downward spiral. Lisa became distant, and Chris was always busy. They never said they were together, but Jason knew. He had known all along.

He smiles. "Hello Lisa."

"Why.... Why are you doing this?"

"Are you pretending or are you just stupid?"

"What are you talking about?"

"Lisa, I love you. I've *always* loved you," tears are in his eyes, "but you never paid any attention to me. I was always the friend, nothing more."

Lisa stands up. "That's not true, you were more. You were my *best* friend..."

He slaps her and she falls back onto the bed. Her cheek reddens where he had hit her. She breaks out in sobs. Jason removes his cap, throwing it onto the ground. He runs his fingers through his hair. There's blood speckled on his pale forehead. It isn't his blood.

"I thought you were smarter than this. The best friend card? Do you think that's how you're going to get out of this? Don't you think Chris tried the same thing? You want to know how that worked out for him?"

Lisa wipes tears from her cheeks. "What did you do to him?"

Jason walks over to her, and she cowers back onto the comforter. He places his arms above her shoulders and straddles her. He's staring intently into Lisa's eyes, but her gaze appears to be focused elsewhere, locked on the gun peeking out from his waistband.

"It all started when we got in a fight, about you, of course. He had the audacity to say that I was crazy. Can you believe it? Crazy..."

Lisa reaches for his gun and yanks it from his waistband. He presses his elbow against her forearm, pushing all his weight down, but she manages to pull her hand up. Her fingers awkwardly pull the trigger. He winces as the bullet tears through his thigh.

Genuine shock is in his eyes. "Why would you do that?"

"Chris was right, you *are* crazy!"

Suddenly, his hands are around her throat. She pulls the trigger again and another bullet enters his flesh. He squeezes tighter and she drops the gun. She claws at his face, gasping for breath. Tears are in both of their eyes. Anger fuels him and love compels him. He has no choice, as there's no coming back from this. She had made her choice and he had made his. Her lips turn blue, and her arms fall limp. She isn't fighting anymore, she's dead.

Jason sits there for several minutes, unmoving, his hands still around her throat. Blood seeps through his dark-colored jeans. Tears fall from his cheeks onto her. The pain he feels in his body is nothing compared to what he feels in his heart. The emptiness that shadows him is one that is only felt from loneliness. Now, Jason is completely and utterly alone. Sure, he has acquaintances and family, but he has lost his closest friend and the love of his life all in one night. He had hoped it would've been different. Perhaps in a different life it could've been. If only he could go back in time, he would've never introduced her to Chris. Surely, that was where he went wrong. His one mistake.

His One Mistake was first published in Broken by Design: A Short Story Collection in June 2021.

20

Two of the Same

It's a Friday night and the Alpha Tau Omega fraternity house is packed full of drunk college-aged kids. The interior of the house is illuminated by rope lights in various neon colors. In the corner of the living room, sitting on a worn, faux white leather couch is Dorian. Dorian is a tall, socially awkward twenty-four-year-old. His boyish face is framed with golden-blond curls. Light freckles are dusted across his cheeks. He's wearing a *Deadpool* t-shirt and jeans, and unlike the seventy or more co-eds in the old house, Dorian is not a student at the university.

"Of course, I'd find you in the corner," Matt says.

Matt is Dorian's closest friend as well as his roommate. Matt is attending the university, studying marketing and minoring in Spanish. He is a pledge of the Alpha Tau Omega fraternity. His chocolate brown hair is cut short and thick-framed glasses sit atop his thin nose. He offers a red plastic cup filled with cheap beer to Dorian.

"Thanks."

Dorian takes a sip and his lips purse uncontrollably. *Keystone Light, of course*. He rolls the cup in his hand.

"You know I brought you here to get you out of your shell and meet some people, preferably girls," Matt looks around the room, "and I think there's quite a few here."

Dorian sighs, but Matt doesn't appear to notice. *If only you knew*. After working an eight hour shift at the factory, his interest in finding someone was less than being at the party in the first place.

"Matt, hey!"

A girl approaches. Her short hair is curled and a bow rests atop her head. Her thin frame is hidden by an oversized t-shirt, its bright orange fabric is a stark contrast to her brown skin.

"Phoebe," Matt throws his arms around her. "It's good to see you! I feel like I haven't seen you in forever. How have you been?"

"I've been good. Congratulations on the pledge."

"Thank you."

She peers over at Dorian. "Who's this?"

"My roommate. Phoebe this is Dorian."

"Hi Dorian."

He slightly raises his cup in response.

"If you two will excuse me, I need to go get a refill. I'll be back," Matt says.

Dorian resists the urge to groan as Matt walks off with a full cup. *Of course he's up to his usual shenanigans*. Matt always tries to set Dorian up with a girl whenever they go out together. For someone who hasn't had a girlfriend for as long as

Dorian has known him, he is awfully persistent. Phoebe takes a seat next to him and smiles. Her fruity perfume is strong enough to smell over the beer and sweaty odors in the air.

"Why haven't I met you before?"

Dorian shrugs his shoulders. "You'd have to ask Matt."

"Come on, we both know Matt's type. Besides, I'd rather talk to you."

Phoebe scoots closer to him and smiles. She places her hand on his thigh and Dorian tenses up. He quickly pushes her hand off.

She frowns. "I'm sorry."

"No, I'm sorry," he stands up. "I don't belong here, but it was nice to meet you, Phyllis."

"Phoebe," she corrects.

"Right."

Dorian pushes his way out of the living room, past the couples making out, those screaming at the party games, and the few people who are passed out on the stained floor. He steps outside onto the porch and sighs heavily. It's cooler outside and the quiet is a welcome retreat.

"Not your scene either?"

Dorian turns to see a handsome stranger standing at the edge of the porch, smoking a cigarette.

"No, not really," Dorian says.

The man flicks his cigarette towards the overgrown yard that's littered with beer cans. He's taller than Dorian and more muscular. His black hair falls past his ears. He's dressed in jeans, a white t-shirt, leather vest, and combat boots. Dorian's heart rate increases as the man's striking blue eyes lock with his.

"Why'd you come then?"

"Roommate drug me along. You?"

"Free beer," the man smiles. "My name is Kalen. I'm assuming you're not a frat guy?"

Dorian laughs. "What gave it away? I'm Dorian."

Kalen puts the cigarette out on the porch and offers his hand to Dorian. His skin is warm, and Dorian can't help but blush as he shakes his hand.

"How would you feel about going somewhere with better beer and less morons?" Kalen asks with a sly smile.

"Where'd you have in mind?"

***

Kalen's bedroom is small and dark. The walls are painted a blood red and the sheets, curtains, and most of the furniture are black- making the room appear even smaller. Dorian zips up his pants while a shirtless Kalen walks in carrying two bottles of *Dos Equis*. From his stomach to his neck, his skin is covered by black and grey tattoos. He hands one of the beers to Dorian and sits down on the bed beside him.

"I thought you said there would be better beer?" Dorian asks.

Kalen shrugs. "Maybe it was all a ruse to get you here and have my way with you."

"Sure," he rolls his eyes. "I forgot to ask you earlier, are you a student?"

"Yeah, I was, but I'm taking a break. Trying to figure out life I suppose. Are you?"

"No, I'm not a student, but in regards to life, I'm trying to figure that one out too."

Dorian's phone buzzes from inside his pocket, but he ignores it. Matt has already texted him several times asking him where he was, but he didn't want to respond. He knows Matt is going to give him a hard-time about leaving the party early, and he wants to put off the lecture for as long as he can.

"You need to get that?" Kalen asks.

He shakes his head. "Just my nosy roommate. He's probably wondering why I ditched him and one of his friends he was trying to set me up with. I'm sure she is a nice girl, but she's not what I'm interested in."

"Ah, I see," Kalen takes a sip of beer. "I take it he doesn't know?"

"He doesn't."

Dorian sighs. It isn't like he's purposely keeping his sexuality from Matt, he just hasn't found the right time or the right way to tell him. Part of him is afraid their friendship would change if he told him. He knows Matt isn't the type to judge someone, but he still struggles with the possibility of it happening. After all, his mother had told him after he came out that she already knew and everything was fine; however, she cut off all contact with him only several weeks after he told her.

"So, you're saying he doesn't know you're gay and doesn't know you left the party with a complete stranger? Isn't that dangerous?"

"I don't know, should I be worried about being alone with you?"

Kalen laughs and slaps his leg. "Relax man, I'm only teasing."

"I know, don't worry."

Kalen reaches out to him and their fingers interlace. "I'm glad I ended up going to that stupid party after all."

"Me too," Dorian makes a face as he fights the urge to yawn. He's not even halfway finished with his beer, but the long day is finally catching up with him.

"You okay?"

"Yeah, but I think I'm going to go ahead and head out. I'm tired," Dorian says.

"Already? You haven't even finished your beer."

"I'm afraid so. Thanks for having me over though, I had a great time- way better than what I would've had at the stupid party."

"Wait, one more thing before you go," Kalen unlocks his phone and hands it to him. "Can I have your number? I'd like to see you again- if you'd be interested."

He smiles. "Of course."

***

It's a little after midnight when Dorian returns to his apartment. He hadn't been able to fight off the yawns on the car ride back to his place and is even more tired than he was before. He's fairly certain he can actually hear his bed calling his name. Matt is sitting in the faux leather recliner in the living room, scrolling through his phone, and stands up as soon as Dorian walks inside. He has a nervous expression on his face.

"Where have you been?" Matt asks.

"I met someone at the party and went to their place for a few hours. Why what's wrong?"

"Nothing," Matt sighs. "I was just worried, that's all."

"It's okay *Mom*, I'm fine," Dorian says.

Matt doesn't look reassured or amused by his words. Despite his overwhelming urge to sleep, Dorian walks over and slumps down on the couch. Matt sits back down, appearing to study his appearance.

"Phoebe said you got upset and stormed off, when I couldn't find you I started thinking something bad might have happened like you got drunk and were taken somewhere."

Dorian laughs. "You should know me well enough that if someone had taken me it would only have been a matter of time before they brought me back. I'm not that interesting."

"Can you be serious for one second? You're a great catch, but if you don't put yourself out there you will always be alone."

"I know you're drunk, but you're being ridiculous," Dorian stands up. "I need sleep, we can talk about my love life in the morning when you're sober."

Matt stands up and steps towards him. His breath reeks of beer. "No, I want to talk about this right now. I've been sitting here and thinking about things and it's just not adding up"

"Fine. Say whatever you have to say."

"Why is it that every time I set you up with a nice girl you make up some excuse and blow her off? I find it hard to believe that you would turn down a great girl like Phoebe. She's smart, beautiful, and ambitious- what more could you need?"

Heat rushes to the back of Dorian's head. "Why don't *you* go out with her if you think she's so damn great?"

Matt opens his mouth to say something, but doesn't. The air around them is tense and heavy. The only noise in their entire apartment is the ceiling fan as it slowly rotates above them. Dorian realizes his hands are balled into fists and forces them to relax at his sides.

"If you're not going to say anything, I'm going to bed," Dorian says.

"I need to tell you something," Matt's voice is barely above a whisper. "I'm gay."

Dorian isn't sure he heard him correctly. *How can Matt be gay?* There was no hint, not even an inkling from the day they met, that he was gay too- or was there? All the times he and Matt had gone out, Matt had spent his time trying to set him up with a girl; however, Matt himself had never shown interest in anyone- not even the girls who had practically thrown themselves at him. Phoebe's words echo in his head, "We both know Matt's type."

Dorian starts laughing uncontrollably and Matt furrows his brow.

"Why is that funny?"

Dorian tries to regain his composure, but can't. All this time, he has been worried about keeping his secret from someone who shared the same secret. How could he have missed this? Matt angrily steps forward, tears in are in his eyes as he shoves Dorian back.

"Stop laughing at me."

Dorian throws his hands up and caught Matt's before he could push him again. His face is red from laughing so hard.

"Listen to me for a second. I'm not laughing at you for being gay, I'm laughing at myself."

"Why?"

"Matt, you don't understand," a chuckle escapes Dorian's lips. "I'm gay. I haven't told you because I was afraid of how you'd react, or if it would change our friendship."

Matt's mouth falls open. "Are you being serious?"

"Yes."

Matt is quiet for a moment before bursting into laughter. Dorian throws his arm around him and pulls him into a tight embrace. He can't help but start laughing again with Matt, seeing the irony of it all- the both of them keeping the same secret for the same reason.

Two of the Same was first published in Broken by Design: A Short Story Collection in June 2021.

21

Miracle

"Jonathon wake up," Nora nudged her snoring husband. Their bedroom was dark, with the only light coming from the nightlight plugged into the wall. She turned on the lamp sitting on her nightstand and nudged him again. Slowly he opened his eyes.

"What is it?" it was a little after four in the morning and his voice was slurred with sleepiness.

"I felt a kick."

Jonathon sighed and closed his eyes. "You were probably dreaming. Just go back to bed."

She yanked the covers off him and threw them onto the shag carpet. He grumbled something under his breath and pulled the pillow over his head.

"I'm being serious, I wasn't asleep," she rubbed her stomach. "I felt her kick."

Jonathon moved the pillow over and sat up. He studied her appearance. His eyes lingered on her hand on her stomach. It was like he was searching for the right words to say and figuring out how to say them. This was a delicate matter after all.

"Nora, honey, you had a miscarriage two weeks ago. I'm sorry, but you couldn't have felt her kicking because she's gone. Please go back to sleep, we have to be up in a few hours to pick your mother up from the airport."

Tears filled her eyes. "I know what I felt."

"I'm not going to argue with you about this right now."

He laid down again, but with his back turned to her. Nora leaned over to turn the lamp off when she felt a small tap on her stomach. A few seconds later there was another one.

"Jonathon, she's kicking again," Nora grabbed his hand and pressed it to her stomach, "Wait for it, I'm not making this up."

As if to humor her in order to actually get some sleep, he obliged. His eyes widened as there was movement in her abdomen. He yanked his hand away as the second thud danced underneath his fingertips.

"Isn't this wonderful?" Nora smiled as a tear rolled down her cheek.

Jonathon got out of bed and grabbed his phone off the nightstand. His fingers were shaky as he struggled to unlock it.

"What are you doing?"

"I'm calling 9-1-1," he said.

"Why?"

He looked at her with a mixed expression of horror and shock. "Nora there has to be something seriously wrong with you for this to be happening. I don't know what that is, but it's not our Annabelle inside you."

"Stop acting crazy, you're scaring me," she grabbed his phone and threw it across the room. "It's nothing to be concerned about- this is a *miracle*!"

"You're the one that's acting crazy! Do you not remember seeing *her*? Among the blood and everything else, that was our baby."

Nora slapped him across the face as hard as she could, and he stumbled back. "Don't you ever talk about Annabelle like that again. Do you hear me?"

He appeared dumbfounded. Nora had never been a violent person, but ever since the start of the pregnancy he had noticed a different side of her- everyone had. She was moody, quick-to-anger, and rarely slept.

"It's her first pregnancy, nothing to be concerned about," the doctors had reassured him. They had assumed he was a doting husband, worried about his lovely wife and their unborn baby. They didn't know about his year-long affair with his secretary or how he had only stayed with Nora because of the baby. Now that she was gone, there wasn't anything holding him back.

"Nora, I need you to calm down and let me call someone so we can make sure you're okay. Alright?"

Nora didn't respond. She was humming softly as she stroked her stomach. The movements had grown more frequent and larger in size. If she had bothered to lift up her night gown, she would've seen the blackness against her pale skin and how it grew with each passing second.

Miracle was first published in Broken by Design: A Short Story Collection in June 2021.

22

More than a Coffee

"That'll be $5.63," the cashier said.

It was a Wednesday morning, and the coffee shop was as busy as usual. The line was wrapped around the interior of the building and spilled out onto the sidewalk outside. The patrons ranged from college kids to businesspersons. Cordelia could've been mistaken for a college student who had just pulled an all-nighter studying for an exam. Her curly brown hair was doused in dry shampoo, yesterday's mascara sat on her eyelashes, and she was dressed in sweatpants and a t-shirt. She fished her wallet out of her tote bag and handed the cashier her credit card. She sipped her vanilla latte, flinching as it burned the roof of her mouth. The cashier ran her card and the machine beeped.

"Ma'am your card was declined."

Her lips pursed. "Can you try it again?"

The cashier took a deep, agitated breath and swiped the card again. The machine's shrill beep signaled another decline. Sweat beaded on Cordelia's forehead. *Didn't I just pay it off?* She couldn't recall the balance, but surely it was less than a thousand dollars. With her rent due next week and her savings dwindling with each passing day, it *had* to be. Cordelia looked to the growing line behind her. There were several impatient expressions in the crowd.

"Do you have another form of payment?"

"Yeah, sure." She opened up her wallet again, dumping out her loose change. "Sorry, I've got it, hang on…"

"Here, I'll cover it," a man said.

Cordelia turned around. He was tall, over six feet, and sported a black suit. Sunglasses sat atop his blond hair. His eyes were a striking emerald-like green. He reached over Cordelia and handed his credit card to the cashier. His cologne was strong and earthy, but not overbearing.

"Thank you," Cordelia said.

He winked at her. "Don't worry about it."

The heat rushed to her cheeks. She gathered her loose change and retreated to a corner table by the window. Several of the patrons watched her, their eyes glanced in another direction when she met their gaze. Her stomach churned and the idea of a latte wasn't appealing anymore. She regretted even leaving her apartment. At least at home she could've sat on the couch and hunted for jobs without being judged by anyone except for her roommate's cat. She retrieved her laptop computer from her bag and set it on the table. As soon as she opened it up, the stranger took the vacant seat across from her. The strong aroma of his coffee overpowered his cologne.

"Hello again," he said.

"Um, hi." Cordelia chewed on her lower lip. "Listen, I can totally pay you back for my coffee, I know I have cash here somewhere."

He put his hand up. "That's not necessary".

"You sure?"

"Positive. My name is Anderson by the way, but most people call me Andy." He extended his hand to her. She hesitated before shaking it.

"Cordelia."

"Nice to meet you Cordelia... Listen, I don't want to come off as creepy or stalker-like, but I've seen you in here a few times. This isn't the first time you've had issues paying for your coffee, is it?"

Great, I wonder how many people have noticed. Cordelia looked down at the table. As a recent graduate of Northwestern University, she had been struggling to find a stable job so she could afford to apply to graduate school and pursue a master degree in social work. It didn't matter that she had graduated with honors, as most employers were interested in experience rather than a four-year degree, even for a simple desk job. To make matters worse, she was let go from her waitressing job at a local café. She had worked at the café for almost a year, but with her boss going through a divorce, he had to make some budget cuts, and her job was one of them. It wasn't the best paying gig, but it had been enough to keep her afloat.

"I mean, yes... but I'm, um, working on it."

"Would you be interested in a job?"

Her mouth fell open. "What?"

"You know, one of those things people do Monday through Friday, eight to five, sometimes nine to six."

"Thank you for clarifying." She rolled her eyes.

"Not a fan of jokes? I get it. I'll be frank with you. I lost my personal assistant last week and I don't have a lot of time to find someone to replace her. Actually, I need someone by the end of the day today really."

"I don't understand. Why would you want to even offer *me* a job? You don't know anything about me."

"To be honest, none of my interviewees so far have stood out and I'm running out of time. Plus I figured we were both in a bind here and could help each other out." He looked down at his diamond encrusted Rolex watch. "Shoot, I'm going to be late. I have to go, but I hope you'll consider my offer. We can hash out the details later."

He retrieved a business card out of his pocket and passed it to her. Before she could protest, he was already gone, out of the coffee shop and running down the street. She looked at the plain card. It read, "Anderson J. Glass, Attorney at Law," with his phone number typed below it. *That explains the Rolex.* She set it down on the table and turned her attention back to her laptop. *Indeed* opened up to where she had left off the night prior, four pages deep into an administrative assistant job search. She squinted as she read one of the position's description. *Didn't I already apply to this one?* Maybe it was due to the lack of caffeine in her system, or due to the fact she had already applied to at least one hundred different jobs in the past few days, but they were all starting to sound the same.

Cordelia sighed as she shoved her laptop back into her bag and stood up. If she had been alone in her apartment, she would've screamed. She grabbed her latte and turned to leave, but hesitated. Anderson's card was face down on the end of the table. She considered leaving it, but slipped it into her pocket in case she changed her mind. A chill ran down Cordelia's spine as she exited the coffee shop. It was a little above fifty-degrees Fahrenheit and the wind was merciless. The typical Chicago scent, a mixture of gasoline, hot-dogs, and sweat from the tourists, was prevalent. Car horns, sidewalk chatter, and the crosswalk signals were deafening. Cordelia tossed the latte into a bin and started the three-block journey back to her apartment.

She never imagined she would be to the point that she couldn't even afford a coffee, let alone a stranger taking enough pity on her to offer her a job. She could hear her grandmother, telling her how proud she was of her for moving half-way across the country to pursue her dreams. She was, at one time, considered the one who was going to make it. Where did it go wrong? It wasn't like she was using her student loan money to go out and party every weekend or splurging on things she didn't need with her former paycheck. She had been responsible, or at least *she* considered herself responsible.

Hank, Cordelia's elderly neighbor, sat on the outside steps in front of her apartment building. A thick, afghan blanket was draped over his shoulders. In one hand he held a quarter, his other a scratch-off lottery ticket. The smell of whiskey and stale cigarette smoke clung to him.

"Morning, Delia. Do you think today is going to be *the* day?" his voice was hoarse.

Cordelia forced a smile. "I sure hope so."

He rubbed the coin against the card, an expectant look in his eyes, as Cordelia ascended the stairs. The building's walls were thin. It invited in the cold outside air as well as Hank's loud displeasure of yet another, losing ticket. The halls echoed with her footsteps, muffled televisions, and conversations intended to be kept behind closed doors. While the building was rich with history, it was lacking in privacy. The thought of the entire complex knowing her struggles was hard to stomach; however, most of the tenants pretended to be oblivious in regards to others' business, so Cordelia tried not to think about it.

Her apartment was on the third floor at the corner of the hallway. A faded welcome sign, courtesy of Hobby Lobby, was hung on the door. As soon as she opened the door, the smell of lavender enveloped her. Sebastian, her roommate's black cat, jumped off the snagged fabric couch and ran over to her. He purred as he rubbed against her legs. Cordelia pulled Anderson's card out of her pocket and examined it. This little card could be the answer to her prayers, but it could also be a one-way ticket to ending up as an unsolved murder mystery on *Dateline*. With her luck, it would be the latter.

"Back already?" Margaret asked.

Margaret, an up-and-coming tattoo artist, was Cordelia's longtime friend and current roommate. She stood in the kitchen, whisking pancake batter and fresh blueberries in a mixing bowl. She was the complete opposite of Cordelia: her short hair was dyed pink, tattoos covered almost every inch of her pale skin, and she was successful both financially and professionally. Cordelia slipped the card back into her pocket and took a seat at the kitchen counter. Sebastian followed her, still purring, and sat down by her feet.

"Yeah, I didn't feel like being out."

"You want some pancakes?"

Cordelia shook her head. "I'm not really hungry."

"Suit yourself."

Margaret poured the batter onto the griddle in two imperfect circles. In spite of her chipper mood, her lips were pursed and eyebrows drawn together. The air in the room felt suffocating.

"Everything okay?" Cordelia asked.

"Couldn't be better... I just, got some news about the job I applied for. The one I told you about, remember?"

Cordelia remembered all too well. Margaret had brought up several weeks ago that she was looking for a new tattoo parlor to work at. It didn't seem like a bad idea, Margaret was talented artist, and needed a shop where she would be in higher demand and could build a loyal clientele. Her current employer, located in a shoe-box-sized building downtown, catered more to the drunk, get-a-tattoo-on-a-whim kind of customer, than the regular ink enthusiast. The problem with the job she was interested in was the location, Atlanta.

"They offered me the job, and want me to start in two weeks."

"That's.... great." Cordelia swallowed the massive lump in her throat. "When do you leave?"

"I haven't accepted the job *yet*. I wanted to talk to you first before making any decisions."

"Why? This is your dream job."

"Because if I leave now, you'll be left in a bind. There's only one more month left on the lease. I don't know if I could find another apartment or roommate within such a short span of time."

Margaret forced the spatula underneath one of the pancakes. It was too soft, and tore as she flipped it over.

"Margaret, don't be silly, go call them right now. I would never let you put your life on hold because of me."

"I can't just abandon you..."

"Yes, you can. I will be fine. I actually accepted a job offer today."

"What? Really?"

Cordelia nodded and smile crept onto Margaret's face. She dropped the spatula and ran over to Cordelia, frightening Sebastian. He fled to the living room as Margaret pulled her into a tight embrace.

"Thank you so much! I'm going to give them a call real quick! Can you finish the pancakes?"

Before she could even respond, Margaret was out of the room. Cordelia sighed and walked over to the griddle. Margaret's door was closed but her excitement was evident from the inaudible phone conversation that seeped through the walls. She was happy for Margaret, but part of her wished she hadn't taken the job, or at least stayed through the entire lease. Surely by then Cordelia would not only have a job, but perhaps a different roommate to help with the rent as well. Even if Cordelia did accept Anderson's offer, she had no details of the salary and could be unable to afford an apartment on her own anyway; however, any form of income, no matter how insignificant, would be better than nothing. The smell of burnt batter filled the air.

"Shit." Cordelia turned the griddle off and shoveled the blackened pancakes onto a plate.

Margaret came out of her room, smile still beaming, as Cordelia walked to the door. Anderson's card felt heavy in her pocket, and her nausea was tenfold.

"Where are you going?" Margaret asked.

"To call my new boss."

***

Anderson's office was located in downtown Chicago, a few blocks away from the courthouse. Cordelia arrived bright and early on Friday morning with a new-to-her briefcase she had picked up at the thrift store, a sack lunch, and her resume. She wasn't sure what an assistant would wear, so she had chosen a simple button up blouse and black pencil skirt. Her hair was tamed with a hair tie. She stood outside the office, clutching her briefcase as she waited. Five minutes turned to ten, ten to twenty, and after thirty minutes, a short and chubby woman walked out of the office. She had an I-would-rather-be-anywhere-else-than-here expression on her face.

"Can I help you?" she asked.

"Hi, yes, well, maybe. I'm Andy's new assistant." Cordelia shot her hand out to her, but the women didn't take it.

"Right, Mr. Glass told me he hired someone to take Sharon's place." She sighed. "Please follow me."

Cordelia followed her inside, careful not to seem too eager. Her nerves were electric as the woman gave a quick tour. The office featured a small receptionist area, a room for Anderson to meet with clients, a bathroom not available to the public, a closet-size breakroom, and then Anderson's office. It was designed with dark grey flooring and charcoal-colored walls. The few prints on the walls were abstract black and white paintings that could've been done by a five-year-old.

The woman knocked on Anderson's door. "Mr. Glass, your new assistant is here."

"You can let her in, Helen, thank you."

Helen opened the door, not even enough room for a cat to squeeze through, and walked off to rejoin her chair at the reception desk. Cordelia took a deep breath and forced a smile. She wasn't going to let Helen, or anyone else for that matter, dampen her spirits. Anderson was sitting behind a large mahogany desk, hiding behind his two computer screens and a thick stack of papers. The walls and floor were the same dreary shade as the rest of the office, but the walls were absent of any art. Only his college diplomas, all held in intricate wooden frames, were hung up. A second desk, smaller than his, sat in the corner. It had a single computer sat up and a framed picture left behind by the previous assistant.

"I'm glad you decided to join us." He smiled, but it appeared somewhat forced. "Please take a seat."

Cordelia sat down in the faux leather chair on the other side of his desk and placed her briefcase on her lap. She unlatched it and pulled her resume out while Anderson clicked on the keyboard. He seemed tired compared to when she had met him. His hair was unruly, and he had bags underneath his eyes. Cordelia set her resume at the edge of his desk and after a moment he picked it up.

"What's this?"

"My resume."

He set it back down. "That's not necessary."

"How will you know if I'm fit for the job without giving it at least a glance?"

"Listen, I'm going to be one-hundred percent honest with you here," he rubbed his temples. "It's a pretty simple job. If I need something, you go get it. If I have somewhere important to be, you make sure I get there on time. I need you to know my schedule by heart- down to the very last, insignificant coffee break. Helen has my itinerary up front for you, along with a card for approved purchases. That being said, you are allowed and expected to use the card for yourself as well when getting things like coffee or lunch."

"So, I'm basically at your beck and call?" she wasn't able to hide the disappointment in her tone.

"No, I wouldn't go as far to say that. Anyway, today I need you to go to the courthouse and pick up some documents regarding a case I'm working on. They already know you're coming so it shouldn't be an issue. I'd like you to bring a coffee on the way back as well. I expect you back in half an hour and not a minute later. Understood?"

Cordelia nodded, but she had a million questions running through her mind. Where exactly in the courthouse did she need to go? Was there a specific coffee shop preference he had in mind or would any old Starbucks do? Not to mention she still had questions about the job itself. She had no idea if the job was considered full or part-time, if benefits were an option or a ballpark figure of the salary. He had assured her over the phone she would be, "Well compensated," but didn't go into details or numbers. Quite frankly, with Margaret leaving, she *needed* a job and the details weren't as important as the job itself.

Anderson looked at her. "Are you waiting for something?"

"No." She stood up. "Sorry."

Her face was flushed when she left his office, but she hoped Helen wouldn't notice. Part of her had hoped this was going to be more exciting than some ordinary desk job, given Anderson's career; however, it appeared she was going to be nothing more than a glorified errand runner. She was half-way to the door when Helen cleared her throat. Cordelia stopped and turned to her.

"Forgetting anything?" Helen gestured to the thick black folder on the counter with a credit card sitting on top of it.

"Right, thanks."

She rolled her eyes. "Wouldn't it be nice if he had actually hired somebody qualified? Maybe next time..."

"Excuse me?"

Helen didn't say anything, as if she hadn't heard her or didn't care to. Cordelia grabbed the folder and slipped the card into one of its pockets. She didn't attempt to say anything else to Helen before she walked out the door.

It was windy outside, and Cordelia hugged the folder to her chest as she walked. The sidewalks were busy and she had to weave her way through the crowd. She had passed the courthouse a few times, but never went inside or paid it any attention. It was a massive building with a white stone exterior and hundreds of windows. The inside was daunting with people swarming around like wasps. Anderson had said the courthouse, but not specifically *where* inside the courthouse. Out of habit, she reached for her phone in her skirt pocket before realizing it was locked up in her briefcase back at the office.

"Shit," she muttered.

"Can I help you?" a young security guard asked. He must've known by her lost puppy like expression that she needed help.

"I really hope so. I'm Andy—I mean Anderson Glass' new assistant. I was sent to retrieve some documents for a case he is working on."

"I wish I could say I'm surprised he has another new assistant." He rubbed his chin. "You're going to want to go to the clerk's office. It's on the second floor, first office to your right."

"Thank you, you have no idea how helpful this is."

She maneuvered her way through the chaos, up the stairs and to the clerk's office. Her small spark of hope fizzled out as soon as she walked inside. The line to the counter was worse than the typical line inside her favorite coffee shop and appeared slower.

"You have got to be kidding me."

The round clock on the wall read nine-fifteen. She had less than twenty minutes to get back to the office.

Cordelia tapped the elderly woman's shoulder who was in front of her. "Um, would you mind if I cut in front of you?

My boss expects me back soon, and it's my first day, so I *really* need to make a good impression."

The old woman snorted, and turned back around without a word. Cordelia felt the heat rush to the back of her head. *Great. Make that my first and last day on the job.*

"You can cut in front of me if you'd like?" a man towards the front of the line offered.

"Really?" she asked.

He nodded. Afraid he might change his mind, she hurried over and stepped in front of him. Her heartrate increased, but it had more to do with the stranger's looks than her approaching deadline. He was tall, like Anderson, but slimmer. His skin was tan, and his dark eyes matched his hair. Dressed in a suave suit, he looked more like a model than assistant to a lawyer.

"Thank you so much! You are a life-saver, like, seriously, I owe you big time."

"Don't mention it." He cracked a smile that made Cordelia's heart skip a beat. "I don't think I've seen you around here before. My name is Vincent."

"This is my first time, I just started working as a lawyer's assistant. My name is Cordelia, but my friends call me Delia."

"Nice to meet you, Delia. How about a drink sometime?"

For once, Cordelia was speechless. If taking a job from a complete stranger wasn't a one-way ticket to murder-town, grabbing a drink with one surely would be.

"Here." He grabbed her folder and scribbled at the top of the first paper inside. "Think about it, and give me a call."

She was still struggling with what to say as he handed back the folder back to her. Part of her worried he had written on something important. After all, she hadn't even gotten the chance to take a peek at the documents inside yet.

"Ma'am? Ma'am, how can I help you?" the clerk asked.

Cordelia had almost forgotten why she was in the courthouse in the first place. She took a deep breath, and turned to the clerk.

"Yes, I need to pick up some documents for Anderson Glass. He said you would be expecting me. I'm his new assistant, Cordelia Jenkins," she said.

"Do you have any form of identification on you?"

"Yes." Cordelia retrieved her driver's license from her skirt pocket and held it up for the woman to see.

"Right—just one moment." The woman stepped away from the desk and through a side door.

"Oh, so you're Anderson's new assistant?" Vincent chuckled. "He always hires the pretty ones."

Heat rushed to the back of Cordelia's head. She could feel Vincent standing close behind her, his cologne covering her like a shroud. He could probably hear her heart beating out of her chest. She opened her mouth to say something, but nothing came out. Her thoughts were jumbled worse than the alphabet in Campbell's soup. It felt like an eternity before the woman returned. She set a thick pile of documents on the desk that was at least six-inches high.

"It's all of this? How am I supposed to carry this?"

The woman shrugged. "Please sign and date here to verify that you received these."

Cordelia's hand shook as she slapped her signature onto the page and lifted the stack. It was about as heavy as it was awkward to carry. Vincent gave her a parting nod, but she was still speechless. An elderly man was kind enough to hold the clerk's door open for her. She couldn't remember if she had thanked him or not. The only thing she was able to concentrate on was walking and the documents in her arms. Afraid she'd slip down the stairs, her eyes were fixed on each step she took. She knew if she fell, the papers would go everywhere and it would take at least a half-hour just to gather them all back up. Who knows how long it would take to try and put them back in order.

Her gait was more awkward than careful as she headed back towards his office. She was hunched over the documents, and her arms were wrapped around them to the point that they were numb. Her focus was on the path ahead of her and keeping her arms steady. The faces in front of her blurred together, as if her brain couldn't handle processing anything else other than the task at hand. She hadn't checked the clock before she left the courthouse, but she assumed she had less than ten minutes to meet the half-hour deadline. What was so important that they needed to be there within half an hour anyway? Was he naïve enough to believe she could handle this for her very first task?

Luckily for Cordelia, the office door was ajar and she didn't have to fumble with the door handle. Helen was behind the desk with a phone pressed against her ear. She wasn't speaking, but every-so-often she nodded her head and tapped on the keyboard. Cordelia strolled by her, and stopped outside of Anderson's door. She shifted the documents onto her hip and knocked on the door.

"Come in," Anderson said.

He appeared to be in the exact same spot as he was when she left. The same focused, or more-like glazed over, expression was on his face. Cordelia sat the documents down on the edge of the desk and took a step back. She was impressed, albeit surprised, she had made it back within his time-frame. A small, relieved smile sat upon her face.

"Thank you." Anderson smiled for the first time since the coffee shop. "You can bring the coffee in as well."

Cordelia's face fell. *How could I have forgotten the coffee?*

"I assume you located my usual order in the itinerary, and I believe Helen's is in there as well. If not, that's alright. I'm so caffeine deprived right now, I'll drink whatever."

"Yes, no worries—none at all, let me go grab it."

Without waiting for his response, she turned around and rushed out of the office. The nearest coffee shop was about five minutes away, but if she *ran*, surely she could get there and back within a few minutes. Anderson wouldn't even know she had forgotten, and it would make for a funny story later. It was only when she reached the welcome sight of the coffee shop's sign, that she realized she had forgotten the itinerary with not only his order preference but his credit card as well. The folder was nestled underneath the mountain of court documents in his office.

"You have got to be kidding me." Cordelia laughed. It wasn't a joyous chuckle, no, it was the kind of laugh one would follow with tears. She threw her hands up in the air in defeat.

"Are you following me?" a familiar voice asked.

Cordelia turned to see Vincent. His eyes were hidden by sunglasses, but there was no mistaking his deep voice or well-tailored suit. Her gaze fell to the coffee he held in his right hand. Its aroma was strong enough to overtake the gasoline from a nearby taxi.

"Is that black coffee?" she asked.

"Yes," he raised his eyebrow. "Why?"

Cordelia's lips curved into a smile. "Do you remember that drink you offered me?"

He nodded, his expression still perplexed.

"I'm going to need to cash in on that, today—right now, actually."

Before he could protest, she grabbed the coffee and flipped around. Vincent extended his hand as if to stop her, but she was already out of his reach. The coffee sloshed in the cup as she ran.

"I've already taken a few sips." Vincent shook his head. "At least let me buy you a new one."

"There's no time," Cordelia yelled, not bothering to look back. She pushed herself through the crowd and narrowly missed running into the door as she entered the commercial building. Sweat gleamed on her skin and the tie that had previously kept her curls at bay was lost somewhere to the streets. Regardless, her face was beaming with pride. She held her head high and kept her shoulders back, not even bothering to look at Helen as she walked through the office's lobby. Anderson's door was still ajar, and it wasn't apparent if he had moved at all while she was gone.

"Here's your coffee." Cordelia smiled as she handed it to him. "It's black, I hope you don't mind, I forgot the itinerary."

"I actually prefer my coffee black, thank you." Anderson's eyes traveled from the coffee cup to Cordelia. Dark coffee stains were on the lid and matched a few blotches on her blouse.

"Did anything happen I should know about?"

"Nothing out of the ordinary." Cordelia took a seat.

Anderson shrugged his shoulders and took a sip of the coffee. "Alright."

More than a Coffee was first published in BarBar on July 11th, 2025.

23

Forgotten Virtues

Daniel leaned forward in his seat as the Winter Soldier's mask was knocked off, and the camera refocused on Sebastian Stan's face. It didn't matter how many times he had seen the movie, it still held the same nostalgia as the first time he witnessed it in theaters. He jumped as three loud knocks on the door sent his Australian Shepherd into a barking fit, overshadowing Chris Evans as he said, "Bucky?"

Daniel fished for the Roku controller in between the couch cushions, knocking over the popcorn bowl, as his dog scratched at his apartment's front door. The round clock on the wall showed six-twenty in the evening. He groaned, knowing it was Whitney waiting on the other side of the door. He considered staying on the couch, waiting her out, but he had already told her he would be there.

"Daniel." She knocked twice more. "Daniel, I know you're home."

Daniel sighed and forced himself towards the door.

"Panda, go to your place." He pointed to the plush pet bed in the corner. The dog continued to growl, but obeyed.

Daniel unlocked the deadbolt, and opened the door as far as the security chain would allow. His ex-girlfriend was standing on the other side of the door, but she looked like a stranger. Her mousey brown hair was curled, her typically natural face was caked in makeup, and a short, tight dress clung to her small frame. Her left hand toyed with the cross necklace dangling from her neck, and a shoebox rested under her right arm. The box was full of junk: hair ties, old polaroids, and a few trinkets not worth a trip to his apartment.

"What is it?" he asked.

"I have to pee," she said. Red lipstick bled from her thin lips onto her pasty skin.

"Can't you hold it?"

"No." She pouted. "Please, I promise I'll be quick."

Daniel gritted his teeth. Every fiber in his being was screaming at him to shut the door, lock the deadbolt, and turn off all of the lights, hiding in the dark until she left. But how long would that take? Letting her use the bathroom would be easier.

"If I let you use the bathroom you have to leave as soon as you're done."

Whitney smiled. "Of course, not a moment longer, I swear."

He sighed, unlatching the security chain and opening the door. Whitney shimmied past him and made a beeline for the bathroom. Panda growled, but remained on his bed. Looking back, he should've trusted his dog—he had never liked her. Daniel shut the door and bumped his head against the wood. He had been naive to think she would've retrieved the box without bothering him. Although they had been broken up for over two months, she had been relentlessly calling and texting him. He couldn't recall how many times he had told her, "No calls, no texts," but it always fell on deaf ears

Daniel walked back over to the couch and slumped down. He eyed the bathroom door, willing it to open and for Whitney to be on her way and out of his life for good. The air conditioner hummed, but it was otherwise quiet: no footsteps, toilet flush, or running water. He strummed his fingers on the armrest and glanced at the clock—six-thirty. His stomach grew queasier with each elongated minute that ticked on. By six-forty, he was fighting the bile from crawling up his throat.

The door creaked open five minutes later, but Daniel's relief was short-lived.

Whitney was naked.

Arms crossed over her breast, she walked out into the living room. Her gait was the opposite of sultry, and an awkward aura framed her.

"No, no, no." Daniel stood up. "You cannot be doing this."

"I think I understand why you broke up with me, and I get it." With tears in her eyes, she dropped her arms to her sides. "It's been five years. We should've done this already."

Daniel ran to the other side of the couch, his socks slipping on the tile floor. Panda bolted after him as if it was a game. Whitney took another step forward.

"Please, Daniel, I love you."

He grabbed the blanket off the couch and threw it at her before shielding his eyes with his hand. Whitney's lip quivered as the blanket fell to the floor.

"Why won't you look at me?" she asked.

"I am not going to look at you until you put your clothes back on."

"Why?" Her face reddened. "Do you not want to have sex with me?"

"No, I don't and I don't think you want this either."

Whitney broke into sobs and retreated back into the bathroom. She slammed the door behind her, knocking an autographed picture of Emilia Clarke off the wall. It hit the ground with a thud and Panda barked as the glass shards scattered across the floor. Daniel grabbed him before he could run over to investigate.

"Dammit, Whit," he said.

Daniel carried the dog into his bedroom, tiptoeing around the glass, and shut the door behind him. He placed the picture of the dragon queen on his counter before retrieving the broom and dustpan from the kitchen. He watched the bathroom door as he started cleaning up the mess, ready to retreat if Whitney tried anything else. His queasiness was gone, but a dull cramp surged through his abdomen. Daniel dumped the remaining pieces into the trash bin before opening his bedroom door and freeing Panda. The dog sniffed where the glass had been.

He sat back down on the couch and turned off the television. There was no going back to *Captain America: The Winter Soldier* after this. The only thing that could make him feel better at this point was a drink strong enough to erase the image of Whitney's naked body from his mind. Hell he really needed something that could make him forget the past five years with her. Panda jumped up on the couch next to him and curled up.

It was almost seven o'clock when Whitney stepped out of the bathroom. Thankfully, she was fully-clothed. Her arms were wrapped around the box, tightly hugging it against herself.

"What is wrong with you?" Daniel asked.

"I'm sorry," she said. Her eyes, red and puffy, were unable to meet his.

"Why did you think this was a good idea?"

"I don't know. I guess I thought that if we had sex that we could get back together," she said.

"Whitney, no." Daniel stood up. "I did not break up with you because we haven't had sex."

She looked at him, her lip quivering. "Right, but maybe, if we did, you would change your mind."

"No. I need you to understand that nothing is going to change my mind. These two months have been a breath of fresh air. I am happier now just focusing on school work, my job, and my friends than I ever was with you."

"You love your friends more than me," she said.

Daniel didn't say anything. "Whitney, you need to realize that it's over."

"No!" Whitney lunged towards him, throwing the box down on the ground and dispersing its contents across the floor. "It was supposed to be me. You are supposed to be with me."

She screamed as Daniel grabbed her fist before she could punch him. He wrestled with her, crushing the mementos of the life they once shared. Panda jumped off the couch and started barking, nipping at her hands. Whitney lifted her leg, kicking the dog back. Panda whimpered and Daniel pushed her away from him and towards the door.

"If you do not leave, I'm calling the police and filing a restraining order."

"Asshole." She threw her hands down to her sides like a toddler. "This isn't over."

Daniel walked to the door and opened it. "Yes, it is. You need to stop calling and texting me, and this has to be the last time you come here."

Whitney stormed out of the doorway. Daniel closed it before she could say anything else. His hands trembled as he locked the deadbolt and the chain. His heart raced. Panda ran over, carrying one of the forgotten polaroids in his mouth, and sat down next to him. Daniel took the picture into his hand. Panda's teeth had imprinted over Whitney's face, distorting it worse than the makeup had.

"I need to call the guys," Daniel said. "They're never going to believe this."

Photo by Jo Haigwood

Kendal Lou earned her MA in Creative Writing from Saint Leo University in 2024. She enjoys spending time with her dog and three cats, riding her horses, attending comic cons, and competing in barrel races.

www.kendalloudickson.com

Other Books by Kendal Lou Dickson

Lie to Me

Whispers Through the Pines

Learning to Trust Again: A Cat's Tale

www.ingramcontent.com/pod-product-compliance
Lightning Source LLC
Chambersburg PA
CBHW032254310726
48973CB00008B/2403